Their eyes met. "Stunning."

What have I gotten myself into? Morgan didn't see how she would be able to resist him for the next two months. She didn't know if she'd make it through the night. "Thanks. You clean up pretty well yourself." Instead of all black, he had opted for a white jacket. His tuxedo caressed his tall, lean frame, and she had visions of undoing—

Abruptly halting her erotic fantasy, she chastised herself again. She had never lost her mind over a man before and had no intentions of starting now. "I'm ready." Morgan slung the thin strap of her silver evening bag over her shoulder and started for the door. Omar caught her hand. The contact sent an electric current up her arm.

"Morgan, I just want you to know how much I appreciate you taking a chance on me." He bent and placed a soft kiss on her cheek.

She ignored the potency of his cologne and the sensations flowing through her that his kiss invoked and said, "You're welcome. I could say the same for you." They shared a smile. The intensity of his stare made her pulse skip, and she turned away.

Dear Reader,

I had a blast writing Morgan and Omar's story! Morgan loves all things football (as do I). So of course she couldn't resist Omar Drummond's offer or the man himself. But he's having a little trouble keeping things professional, too. Any guesses as to who succumbs first?

In this story, I also touch briefly on PTSD and its effects on Omar's family. In my research, I came across many stories from veterans and their family members, ranging from heartbreaking to hopeful. I also had an eye-opening conversation with my army veteran sister, who graciously shared part of her story. I hope you will consider donating to your local veterans organization.

Thank you for all of your emails and messages. I love hearing from you!

You all have asked about Brandon's story. He's up next and I can't wait for the woman who can take his mind off work.

Much love,

Sheryl

Website: www.SherylLister.com

Email: sheryllister@gmail.com

Facebook: Author Sheryl Lister

Places
in my
Heart

SHERYL LISTER

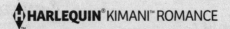

HARLEQUIN® KIMANI™ ROMANCE

Recycling programs
for this product may
not exist in your area.

ISBN-13: 978-0-373-86470-6

Places in My Heart

Printed in U.S.A.

Sheryl Lister has enjoyed reading and writing for as long as she can remember. She writes contemporary and inspirational romance and romantic suspense. She was nominated for a 2015 Emma Award and a 2015 RT Reviewers' Choice Best Book Award, and was named BRAB's 2015 Best New Author. When she's not reading, writing or playing chauffeur, Sheryl can be found on a date with her husband or in the kitchen creating appetizers and bite-size desserts. Sheryl resides in California and is a wife, mother of three daughters and a son-in-love, and grandmother to two very special little boys.

Books by Sheryl Lister

Harlequin Kimani Romance

Just to Be with You
All of Me
It's Only You
Tender Kisses
Places in My Heart
Unwrapping the Holidays with Nana Malone

Visit the Author Profile page at
Harlequin.com for more titles.

For my sister, Sgt. Ramona L. Robinson, US Army veteran.

Acknowledgments

My Heavenly Father, thank you for my life.

To my husband, Lance, my children, family and friends,
thank you for your continued support.
I appreciate and love you!

Gina Golly, you always bring a smile to my face!
Love you much.

A special thank you to the readers and authors I've met
on this journey. You continue to enrich my life.

Thank you to the men and women who serve
in our armed forces. I am grateful for your sacrifice.

Thank you to my editor, Patience Bloom,
for your editorial guidance and support.

A very special thank you to my agent, Sarah E. Younger.
I appreciate you more than words can say.

Chapter 1

He couldn't take his eyes off her. His gaze traveled from her small feet in bright pink tennis shoes, up her long, smooth honey-brown legs and lingered briefly on an apple-round bottom that would make a grown man lose his mind. He continued upward to the grass-stained oversize T-shirt tied at the waist, giving him a glimpse of the gemstone in her belly ring. A ragged ponytail sat at the top of her head with bits of grass and weeds littering the strands that flowed in disarray around her mud-smudged face. Omar Drummond edged closer to the woman. She smelled like...dirt. She was stunning.

A dull thump in the center of his chest jarred him out of his thoughts.

"Yo, Drummond. Get your head in the game," one of his teammates yelled.

"Yeah, Drummond. The object of the game is to catch the football with your hands, not your chest."

He shifted his gaze back to the woman speaking, the focus of his musings. Morgan Gray.

"If this is any indication of your skills," she continued, "the Cobras are in for a long season."

"This is just a backyard scrimmage," Omar said mildly. "My game on the field is just fine. I'm always in the zone. Check last year's stats." He was one of the best tight ends in the league, but his LA Cobras team had lost the conference championship game by one point last season, costing them a coveted trip to the national championship. The loss had nagged at him for weeks, and he vowed that next season they'd bring home the trophy. "Better yet, ask your brother." Morgan's twin brother, Malcolm, was the team's star running back.

Morgan merely smiled while several of the guys snickered.

He moved into his position. "Are we playing or not?"

The game ended a short time later with Omar making the winning touchdown for his team. More good-natured ribbing ensued as everyone traipsed over to recover and relax in the chairs and loungers set up in Malcolm's yard. Malcolm hosted the barbecue for his teammates and their significant others every year before the new season began.

Malcolm handed Omar a beer and lowered himself into the lounger next to him. "You redeemed yourself nicely at the end of the game."

Omar chuckled. "Yeah. Couldn't let your sister call me out like that."

"Morgan has no problems speaking her mind, especially when it comes to football. She's been critiquing my game since I was eight." They laughed. "Your contract is coming up soon, isn't it?"

"In about six weeks."

"Well, with the way you've stepped in as receiver after Colin's injury, Roland should be able to negotiate one hell of a deal." Colin Rush had gone down with a torn ACL, MCL and meniscus two games into last season.

Omar's stomach rolled at the mention of his current agent's name, and he set the beer aside. "We'll see," he murmured. Roland Foster had come highly recommended by several athletes as someone who could secure the best contracts around. After two disappointing experiences with agents, Omar had counted himself lucky when the man had offered representation. True to his reputation, Roland had hammered out a deal that topped the news for weeks. But that was then.

Omar scanned the yard and saw Morgan laughing with

another player's wife. They were the only two women who had joined in the otherwise all-male football game. She had impressed him with her offensive and defensive skills. Not many women—and none he'd dated—would subject themselves to a light tackle football game and not care about being dirty or having messy hair. But Morgan was different, and that turned him on.

"Man, you don't have anything to worry about," Malcolm said. "Roland will make sure you stay with the Cobras as long as you want." When Omar didn't comment, Malcolm leaned forward. "What's up, Drummond?"

"I can't go into details, but I think it's time for a change. And this time, I want to steer clear of anybody involved in league politics. I need somebody else, Mal."

Malcolm studied him for a moment and then said, "My sister is looking to get into the business."

"Is that right? She's an attorney?"

"Yeah. And she's about as far away from *league politics* as you can get."

"So, she knows the game well, huh?"

"As if she's played it all her life," Malcolm said.

Omar had thought that was the case, but hearing Malcolm confirm it solidified in his mind that she might be exactly the person he needed to help him.

"Food's ready," Omar heard someone say.

He came to his feet, eager to end the conversation. Omar got in line with the rest of the guests, filled his plate and crossed the yard to where Morgan sat with her food. His intention had been to talk to her about a business proposition, but as soon as he sat and opened his mouth, two other women joined them and started a conversation about some popular television show. He promptly tuned out and dug into his meal.

"What about you, Drummond?"

His head popped up, and he met Morgan's expectant gaze. "I'm sorry. What did you ask?"

"I asked which show was your favorite—*Scandal* or *How to Get Away with Murder*?"

"I don't watch either show."

Morgan slanted him a look. "Let me guess. You only watch sports or sports news."

"No. I enjoy a good comedy or action movie, but I prefer reading to television."

Surprise lit her eyes. "Reading?"

"Yeah, you know…books."

"Wow, really, Omar? I would've never figured that out," she said teasingly and rolled her eyes. The group laughed.

Omar smiled. She'd called him by his first name, something she had never done before. Their easy rapport gave him hope that she would be receptive to his plan. They finished eating while talking, and afterward, three other guys convinced Omar to join them in a card game. He kept one eye on his cards and the other on Morgan, waiting for a chance to get her alone.

His opportunity came three hands later when he saw her go inside. It took some serious patience to finish the game, especially since his partner seemed to contemplate every round. In Omar's mind it was simple—you either had the card or you didn't.

Marcus Dupree, wide receiver, threw up his hands. "Grant, do you think we could finish this game *before* the season starts? We only have a month."

"My thoughts exactly," Omar mumbled.

"Patience, my brothers," Lucas Grant said. "I have to get my strategy together." The middle linebacker employed the same tactics when watching plays develop and stopping runs between the tackles. Though effective on the field, today it only irritated Omar.

Omar shook his head. Minutes later, he tossed out his

last card and stood. "Somebody else can take my spot. I'm done." Without waiting for a reply, he headed for the sliding glass door that led to the kitchen and stepped inside. The sight of Morgan's long bare legs stopped him in his tracks. She had changed into another pair of shorts that stretched taut over her backside as she reached for something in a cabinet. If he could just get one touch... Omar shook himself and quickly dismissed the notion.

"I see you changed."

Morgan whirled around. "Oh. Drummond, you scared me."

Back to last names again. "Sorry."

She set the glass she had gotten on the counter and went to the refrigerator. "That's okay. I had to shower. I can only take feeling grimy for so long."

It took him a moment to realize she had commented on his previous statement. "I hear you. But you played a good game."

"Are you referring to the interception or the touchdown?" she asked as she poured what looked like iced tea into the glass.

"A little cocky, aren't you?"

She leaned against the counter, wrapped one arm around her middle and took a sip of her drink. "My game speaks for itself. Yours, on the other hand, can use some work."

Omar closed the distance between them and braced his hands on the counter on either side of her. "Is that a challenge?"

She tilted her chin and stared at him intently. "You tell me."

Their faces were inches apart. Common sense told him he should back up, but he couldn't. Not when her full, gloss-slicked lips were calling to him. Without thinking about the ramifications, he crushed his mouth against hers and slid his tongue inside when her lips parted on a startled gasp. She came up on tiptoe and met him stroke for stroke, causing him to groan.

A second later Morgan stiffened and tore her mouth away. She pushed against his chest. "Move."

Omar dropped his arms. "Morgan, I—" She brushed past him, and he reached out to stop her.

She slapped his hand away and kept walking.

"Morgan, wait. I need to talk to you."

"I think you've said enough," she called over her shoulder.

He stared at her retreating back as she stormed out of the kitchen. He cursed under his breath and slammed his hand on the counter. "Brilliant, Drummond. Just brilliant," he muttered. After that stupid move, she most likely wouldn't listen to a word he had to say about his contract now. What had possessed him to kiss her? He had never been able to resist a challenge, and when she got in his face, her sexy, full lips and intoxicating fragrance had stripped him of his good judgment. As much as he wanted a repeat of one of the hottest kisses he'd ever experienced, he needed her expertise more. His desire would have to take a backseat. For now.

Morgan Gray jogged up the stairs, entered the bedroom she always used when she came to her brother's house and closed the door. She slumped against it, closed her eyes and willed her trembling body calm. She couldn't believe Omar had kissed her. Or that she'd kissed him back. It had lasted mere seconds, but the man had managed to unnerve her, something not easily done. *And what a kiss.* She reached up to touch her lips and then snatched her hand away. The man was fine as all get out, and she had seen the legions of women falling at his feet. If he was expecting her to act the same way, he had another think coming.

Morgan jumped slightly when she heard the knock on the door behind her.

"Morgan?"

She opened the door. "Hey, Mal."

Malcolm's brows knitted together. "What's wrong?"

"Nothing. Why?"

"I don't know. I just felt something."

She waved him off and started past him. "I think you make up half this stuff so you can be nosy." No matter how much she tried to discount the whole psychic twin thing, her brother always knew when she was upset or bothered.

He caught her arm. "You know better than that."

"There's nothing wrong. I came up to shower and recover from my awesome game."

Malcolm scrutinized her a long moment, then nodded. "If you say so."

"I say so." Morgan preceded him out of the room and back downstairs, where everyone still sat relaxing and chatting. She walked over to a small group engaged in a domino game and asked to play.

Several times during the rest of the afternoon and into the early evening, she caught Omar staring her way and did her best to ignore him. He'd said he wanted to talk to her, and for a split second Morgan contemplated going over to ask about it. However, memories of that kiss kept her away. She'd have to be dead not to be attracted to him, but she wasn't in the market for a relationship. Especially with another athlete.

Finally the guests trickled out one by one, and she busied herself with retrieving purses and bags, hoping that Omar would be among the first to leave. But he stayed around until only he and one other teammate remained. She went to the kitchen to put away the food and begin the long cleanup process that always followed these gatherings.

Not hearing any noise coming from the family room, she ventured out, thinking everyone had gone.

"Oh, I thought everybody was gone," she said upon seeing Omar and Malcolm engaged in a seemingly serious discussion. "I didn't mean to interrupt."

Omar stood. "You aren't. You're more than welcome to join us."

"Um…that's okay. I'm going upstairs." Their eyes met, silently communicating that they had unfinished business, but she'd had enough for one evening. Morgan turned toward her brother, who slowly came to his feet and divided a speculative glance between her and Omar. "Malcolm, I put away most of the food, but you'll have to tell me where you want the rest when you two are done. Come get me when you're ready."

Malcolm nodded. "We shouldn't be too long."

She tried to keep her eyes focused solely on Malcolm but failed.

Omar smiled. "It was good to see you again, Morgan."

"Same here," she mumbled and fled. She didn't stop until she reached the safety of her bedroom. Once there, Morgan flopped down on the bed and blew out a long breath. Though she shouldn't even have let her mind go there, the only thing she could think about was kissing him again. The demanding way his mouth moved over hers came back with vivid clarity—pillow-soft lips, scorching hot tongue—and every inch of his lean, muscular body had been pressed against hers while his strong hands caressed her back. She wanted to wrap her hands around his sexy locs and keep right on kissing him.

She sat up abruptly at the sound of knocking on the door. Malcolm poked his head inside. "Did I wake you?"

She swung her legs over the side of the bed and stood. "No. Drummond gone?"

"Yeah. It's getting kind of late, so you should stay the night. We can go riding tomorrow."

"Okay." She hadn't planned to spend the night, but Malcolm knew the offer of going for a ride on his motorcycle would definitely make her stay. And clothes weren't a problem since all five siblings kept a stash at each other's houses. All three of her brothers were protective of Morgan and her sister, Siobhan, and didn't like them to be out at night alone. But since Siobhan had gotten married last weekend, responsibility for her safety now fell to her new husband.

She followed her brother back down to the kitchen. "I took care of the side dishes, but wasn't sure what you wanted to do with all this meat." There were trays of ribs, chicken, hot links and salmon.

"I'll freeze some of it for sure, but Brandon and Khalil are coming over tomorrow, so it won't go to waste."

Morgan laughed. "You know Brandon's going to be happy, especially since we aren't having a family dinner tomorrow." Brandon was the second oldest, after Siobhan. Morgan and Malcolm were the youngest. Their tight-knit family still got together at their parents' house for dinner at least one Sunday out of the month.

"Yep. He'll probably take home leftovers. Khalil, on the other hand, will just eat the salmon and vegetables." They both laughed. Khalil was third in line, and the model turned fitness buff ate healthy at least 95 percent of the time. "A couple of guys from the team said they might stop by, too, so I'll send some stuff home with them. Grab some Ziploc bags and let's finish."

She wanted to ask if Omar was one of the guys, but refrained. She was not supposed to be thinking about him. Reaching into the drawer, she got the bags and began filling them.

They worked in silence for a few minutes and then

Malcolm asked, "What's up with you and Drummond?" He came around the island to where she stood adding hot links to one of the bags.

"Nothing."

"So, all that heat the two of you were generating in my family room was nothing. I'm not blind, Morgan. He's usually one of the first to leave, and I couldn't figure out why he stayed longer than usual. Until you came into the room." He angled his head. "Did something happen between you earlier? Like when I found you upstairs?"

Malcolm didn't miss anything when it came to her. "We spoke briefly when I came in for a glass of tea. If this is the part where you tell me he's got lots of women and I should stay away from him, you can save your breath. I know what kind of man he is and I've read the headlines."

He folded his arms and continued to study her. "Actually, I wasn't. But seeing as how you're all on the defensive, maybe I *should* be concerned."

Morgan zipped the bag and pushed it over with the others. "Please. Now, I'll admit the man is fine and has a body that's out of this world, but I have no interest in seeing my face added to his long list of groupies. Been there, done that. And I have enough problems as it is dealing with this lawsuit." She worked as an attorney in her family's home-safety company and had just been appointed the lead on the suit that alleged one of their bathtub safety rails broke and resulted in someone being injured.

"How's that going?"

"I'm not sure yet. We're still waiting on a couple of reports, but it doesn't look good. We could use a miracle right about now. I'm only two years out of law school, and this is my first big case. I don't want to let Daddy down."

He slung an arm around her shoulder and kissed her temple. "Just do your best. That's all you can do."

She leaned into his embrace. "I know. Thanks." Morgan glanced around the kitchen. "Do you need me to do something else?"

"Nah, I'll take care of it."

"You could hire someone to do this kind of thing."

Malcolm shook his head. "You know I don't like a lot of strangers in my house. Having the housekeeper here twice a month is enough."

She smiled. "What time are we riding?"

"I'm sleeping in, so we can go around eleven. Night, sis."

"Good night."

Morgan went upstairs, showered and climbed into bed. She tossed and turned for hours, unable to get Omar's kiss out of her mind. Then she recalled him wanting to talk to her. She could probably ask Malcolm for his number. *No way.* As curious as she was, she knew the best thing would be to forget all about that conversation. And the kiss.

Chapter 2

Morgan sat at her desk Monday morning, poring over the information she had been given on the lawsuit. "Not good, not good," she muttered. A sixty-one-year-old woman had suffered a fractured hip, a broken wrist and a multitude of bruises and contusions. She groaned and lowered her head to the desk. *Why me, Daddy?*

"You okay, Morgan?"

Her head snapped up. "Hey, Brandon."

Her brother Brandon entered and folded his tall body into one of the chairs in front of her desk. "What's wrong?"

She pointed at the stack of papers in front of her. "This doesn't look good for us. Did you see the list of all Mrs. Sanderson's injuries?"

His lips settled in a grim line. "I did, but this has never happened before. We tested and retested those rails before they went to market, and I can't believe one just... just *broke*."

"Me, either, but until I can get a look at it, this is all I have to go on."

"What do you mean? You haven't gotten the rail yet?"

Morgan shook her head. "I requested it and the original packaging, as well as the purchase receipt. As soon as I get it, I'll know more. Of course, their lawyer is insisting a neutral third party be present to make sure I don't tamper with the evidence." Clay Porter reminded her of one of those slick attorneys only out to make money for themselves.

Brandon's brow lifted. "He said that to you?"

"Yes. He's a pompous ass. At our first meeting, the first

thing he said to me was, 'Can you bring everyone some coffee, honey?' I told him I'd ask my secretary to handle it. He had the nerve to laugh when he found out I was handling the case and mumbled something that sounded like it would be his easiest case. It took everything I had not to slap that smug smile off his face."

"I can make sure one of the more experienced attorneys attends the next meeting if you want." Brandon headed up the home safety division of the company and was in line to take over as CEO once their father retired. The company had a smaller division that focused on gym equipment that her brother Khalil designed to make his fitness center more accessible.

"I thought about that at first, but no, thanks. I'll take care of it myself." No way would she let that old weasel intimidate her. "Are we still getting a lot of negative press?"

"Not as much as in the first couple of weeks. But I'll be glad when Siobhan gets back." Siobhan was the PR director and had a way of handling the press unlike anything they had ever seen.

"Me, too. She left Melvin Wilkins in charge, didn't she?"

"Yeah. And Gordon has been in my office four times in the last week complaining since she's been gone." Gordon Samuels worked as a media specialist and had expected to be promoted over Siobhan when the previous director retired. He had been a thorn in Siobhan's side ever since.

Morgan laughed. "I know he was pissed that she didn't leave him in control, especially since Melvin is what, twenty-five, twenty-six, and has been here only two years. Well, if Gordon wasn't still stuck in the nineties, he might've had a chance at the job."

Brandon smiled. "Yeah, right. We all knew that Vonnie would get the job." He stood and walked to the door. "Let me know if you need anything."

"I will. Thanks." Left alone again, she smiled. Her brothers could be a pain in the butt sometimes, but she wouldn't have traded them for the world.

She studied the case for the rest of the afternoon, making notes and flagging the spots where she had questions. She couldn't put her finger on it, but something didn't add up. Glancing up at the wall clock, she frowned. "I can't believe it's almost five already." Morgan leaned back, rotated her chair toward the window and stretched. Her brain was fried and she wanted to go home. But she had to meet with her friend Brooke tonight to finalize their dance production. Brooke Alexander had been Morgan's best friend since ninth grade, when they both had parts in the school's spring dance production. While Morgan had changed directions and opted for law school, Brooke had pursued a successful dance career until injuries from a car accident forced her to quit. With her family's backing, she had opened a thriving dance studio two years ago.

"Somebody's here to see you."

Morgan counted to ten then slowly turned her chair to face the woman standing in her door. The thirty-something administrative assistant had not been happy when she'd been reassigned from one of the senior attorneys to Morgan and, unless the two men were watching, took every opportunity to disrespect Morgan. Like entering the office without calling on the intercom or knocking.

"What can I do for you, Evelyn?"

Evelyn's jaw tightened at Morgan's irritated tone. "There's someone here to see you."

"Who is it?"

"He didn't say, and it's time for me to leave," Evelyn said impatiently.

Morgan slowly rose to her feet and braced her hands on the desk. Leaning forward, she said with a controlled tone, "Let's get something straight. You don't have to like me, but you *will* respect me. Before entering my office, you will use the intercom or knock. I'd hate to have to report you to Mr. Klein. Are we clear?" The woman visibly blanched. Mr. Klein headed the legal department. Morgan smiled. "Now, please show the gentleman in and have a nice evening."

Evelyn gave Morgan a frosty glare and exited.

She lowered her head and drew in several calming breaths.

"Morgan?"

Morgan went still. It couldn't be. Yet when she lifted her head, her gaze collided with the one man she hadn't been able to stop thinking about.

Omar knew he had taken a risk showing up at Morgan's office, but he was desperate. It had taken a lot to persuade Malcolm to share his sister's information, especially since Omar had declined to say what had happened between them. He'd toyed with calling first, but changed his mind because he didn't want to chance her refusing to see him. The woman seated outside Morgan's office, whom he assumed was the assistant, greeted him with a wide smile and an exaggerated sway of her hips as she led him to the office. Omar ignored the not-so-subtle brush of her breasts against his arm when she turned to leave. In his peripheral vision, he noticed the slight rise in Morgan's eyebrow and knew she'd seen it, too. He waited until the woman closed the door before turning to face Morgan.

Morgan folded her arms. "What are you doing here?"

"Hello to you, too," he said.

An embarrassed expression crossed her face. "Sorry. Have a seat."

Omar took the chair opposite her desk. "I apologize for stopping by without calling, but I figured you wouldn't see me otherwise."

"You were probably right. How do you know I won't call security to throw you out now?"

"I don't, but I'm counting on your love of football to work in my favor." They engaged in a stare-down for several seconds until she looked away first.

"How did you know where I worked?"

"Malcolm." She frowned and he added, "If it's any consolation, he adamantly refused to divulge your home address."

"Well, maybe I won't kill him, after all."

He chuckled.

"Since you went through all this trouble, I guess I can spare you five minutes."

Omar knew the mention of football would rouse her curiosity. "I'd like to talk to you about a business proposition."

"What does that have to do with football?"

"My contract is up for renewal in six weeks and—"

"Don't you have an agent? If memory serves me correctly, you have one of the best agents around."

"Things aren't always as they seem."

She sat up straight. "What are you saying?"

"I'm saying it's time for a change, and I'd like you to negotiate my upcoming contract. You're an attorney and, according to your brother, you know football like you've played it all your life."

Her eyes lit up and her mouth fell open. "Are you *serious*? Wait a minute." She sat back again and angled her head. "What about your current agent? Did he dump you or something?"

Omar sighed. "No." There was more to it, but he would only tell her if she agreed to represent him.

Morgan narrowed her eyes. "There are dozens of sports agents out there, and I'm certain any one of them would be happy to take you on, especially with your numbers from last year. Yet you're in my office."

He smiled. "You checked my stats? So, you're admitting I've got game?"

A rush of color darkened her face. "Why me?" she asked, ignoring his questions.

"You want to be an agent, and I need one." He leaned forward and whispered, "And I know you passed the sport's agent certification test. It's a win-win situation for both of us."

"On second thought, I *am* going to kill Malcolm," she muttered.

"I need your help, Morgan. I wouldn't be here if I didn't."

"I have to think about this." She turned slightly in her chair and stared out the window, and then back at him. "You realize I already have a job. And I'm working on a case."

Omar nodded. "I understand, and I have no problems working around your schedule."

"Even on weekends or late evenings."

"Anytime."

"I see." She went back to staring out the window.

He could almost hear the wheels turning in her head. She bit down on her lip, drawing his attention and reminding him how much he enjoyed kissing her.

Finally she angled her head his direction. "I'll agree on one condition."

"What's that?"

"You keep your hands and lips to yourself. No more kisses."

Omar groaned inwardly. There was no way he could go without kissing her. In fact, it had been the first thing on his mind from the moment he saw her today. "Morgan—"

"No. More. Kisses," she repeated.

At this point, he needed her expertise more, he told himself. Not having any other choice, he said, "Fine."

"Good. Then I'll draw up the necessary documents, and we'll meet so you can sign." Morgan picked up a business card, scribbled something on it and handed it to him.

A measure of relief spread throughout his chest. "There's one other thing," he added hesitantly, reaching for the card.

"What's that?"

Rather than give her an extensive explanation up front, he handed her a large envelope.

She took the envelope and removed four stapled sets of papers. She skimmed the documents and frowned. "Two of your endorsement contracts?"

"Yes."

"Why do you have two copies of each one?"

"Go to the flagged pages and you'll see."

Morgan flipped to the pages and compared the two contracts. She did the same with the second contract, and he saw the moment comprehension dawned. She lifted her head. "Are you telling me your agent…?"

He nodded. "I need you to represent me—"

She held up a hand. "No. I can't do both. That would be a conflict of interest."

Omar's jaw tightened. "I don't care. I need someone who's not affiliated with the league to handle this."

Morgan ran a hand through her long curls and sighed impatiently. "Look, Omar. I'll be happy to work with you on your contract, but I cannot represent you in a lawsuit against your current agent. Do you know what people would say? They'd think I was trying to get rid of him for my own purposes. And since my big-mouth brother told you about my desire to be in sports management, you have to know this would kill the slim chance I'd have."

He blew out a long breath. "I know, and I'm sorry.

You're probably wondering why, with all the money I've made, would I be concerned about a hundred and fifty thousand dollars." If his hunch was correct, that dollar figure would increase significantly.

"I'm not wondering at all. It's *your* money. *You* earned it, and no one has a right to take it from you. What about Marcus Dupree's brother, Jaedon? I heard he and another guy opened a law firm a year ago. And from what I understand, he's ruthless in the courtroom."

Omar had met Jaedon and chatted with him a few times, but because Jaedon handled Marcus's contract, Omar assumed the man was just another sports agent. "He's not a sports agent?"

"No. He worked at a prestigious firm at one time, but after winning some big case, he decided to strike out on his own."

"Maybe I'll look him up." He pushed to his feet. "I appreciate you not tossing me out on my butt and hearing me out."

Morgan stood, extended her hand and chuckled. "Yeah, well, you caught me on a good day."

Something about the way she smiled made his heart beat a little faster, and the one thing he wanted to do, he couldn't. He'd made a promise. "Thanks, Morgan. Let me know when and where you want to meet."

Morgan looked at her watch. "I will."

"I'm sorry. Am I keeping you from something?" It had never occurred to him that she might have a boyfriend. And he didn't like the idea one bit.

"It's fine. I'm just meeting my friend Brooke. I'll send her a text to let her know I'll be a few minutes late."

Omar should not have been so happy to hear she didn't have a date, but he was. "If you're leaving, I'll walk you down to the garage." She seemed to weigh her options. Even though they had been focused on business, the heat between them still simmered, and being alone in an elevator might not be the best choice. For either of them. But he didn't care. "It looked like everyone was leaving when I arrived, and I'd rather you not walk down alone."

"Fine. Just give me a minute."

He waited as she shut down her laptop and then stuffed it along with several file folders into a bag.

She glanced over her desk once more. "All right, I'm ready." She slung the bag over her shoulder, then a purse she'd pulled from the drawer, and came around the desk. "Oh, wait. I need to send Brooke a text." Morgan dug out her cell phone and typed something quickly, her fingers moving rapidly on the screen. When she was done, she dropped it back into her purse. "Okay. Let's go."

The outer office was quiet when they passed through and, thankfully, the secretary was gone. Neither spoke as they walked down the hallway, boarded the elevator and rode it to the ground level.

Omar followed Morgan to her car and let out a long whistle. "Muscle car," he said of the Dodge Challenger. "Reminds me of Dom Toretto's car in the *Fast & Furious* movies."

Morgan laughed. "I've always loved fast cars and motorcycles, and this right here," she said, running her hand across the car's black matte finish, "is my baby." She slanted him a look. "You have a problem with women driving fast cars?"

The tone of her voice gave him pause. It was as if she had faced disapproval for her choice in car. "Not at all. I admire a woman who knows what she wants and goes after it, no matter what anyone else thinks." She unlocked the door by remote, and he opened and held it while she got in. "Give me a call when you're ready to go over the contract."

"I will. See you later."

He waved as she drove past him. There was something

downright sexy about a woman in a fast car. It made him curious about what else she liked. Cutting off his train of thought, he reminded himself about their agreement. He could make it. It was only a few weeks. But after the contract negotiations, he planned to do his best to show her that they would be good together, professionally and personally.

Chapter 3

"Sorry I'm late," Morgan said, rushing into the dance studio and dropping her duffel bag on a chair.

Brooke Alexander continued her stretching exercises and smiled. "No problem. I know you're working on a big case."

She lowered herself to the mat across from Brooke. "Yeah, but that's not what kept me at the office."

Brooke stopped midstretch. "No?"

"Omar Drummond showed up at my office unannounced."

"Omar Drummond, as in End Zone Drummond? The pro football player we were all drooling over when he did that men's body wash commercial wearing only a towel, with his locs flowing all around his shoulders?"

"The one and only."

"I can't decide which part of that commercial I liked more, him in the shower with the water streaming over every sculpted ridge of his chest and abs or the full-body shot of him in that skimpy towel."

"The shower," they both said and fell out laughing.

"I wish he'd show up unannounced here...*and* wearing only that towel."

"I bet you do," Morgan said, still chuckling. Then again, she wouldn't have minded seeing him in that towel once more, either. Every part of his deep bronze six-foot-six-inch, two-hundred-fifty-pound body was a pure work of art, all muscle and not one ounce of fat anywhere.

"Well, what did he want?"

"He wants me to negotiate his upcoming football contract."

Brooke sat straight up and her eyes widened. "He's been in the league for a good while, hasn't he? I would think he'd already have an agent."

"He does, but said he needed a change." She kept the other details to herself.

"That's all you used to talk about when we were in high school—being a sports agent. You're finally getting your chance, and without the headache of trying to get the good old boys to take you seriously. Athletes, too, for that matter. Most people starting out have to work their way up to the more established players, but if Omar trusts you, that'll make your road much easier. Are you going to do it?"

"I said I would, but I'm having second thoughts." With all the chemistry flowing between them, it would be too easy for a repeat of Saturday. And she couldn't let that happen.

"You must be out of your mind. The opportunity to live your dream literally drops in your lap, and you get cold feet."

"It's not that."

Brooke folded her arms and waited.

"We had sort of like a…"

"A what? Please don't tell me you and that smart mouth of yours said something crazy."

Morgan lay back on the mat and closed her eyes. "No," she huffed. "He kissed me when we were at Malcolm's house on Saturday."

She pumped her fist in the air and let out a whoop. "Is that all? You go, girl."

Morgan skewered Brooke with a look.

Brooke shrugged. "What's the big deal? You kissed. If you weren't attracted to him, I'd be worried about you."

"Really, Brooke? The big deal is it's a conflict of interest. Besides, you know as well as I do that he has more women than Solomon did in the Bible."

"The right woman will make a man settle down. And how did you two end up in a lip-lock?"

Morgan rolled her eyes and told her what happened in Malcolm's kitchen and the details of his visit earlier. "I said that I would only work with him if there were no more kisses," she finished.

"And he agreed to it?"

"Yes."

A slow smile crept onto Brooke's lips. "I can't wait to see who will be the first one to break that rule. And it *will* be broken. Mark my words."

And that was the crux of Morgan's problem. "Enough about that," she said, changing the subject. "We're supposed to be discussing the dance production."

"Whatever you say," Brooke said, her smile still in place. "Okay. I'm loving your Michael Jackson theme, and the kids are definitely enjoying it. I think they'll be more than ready by showtime. There are a couple more pieces I want to add for the advanced students."

"We need to get my brother-in-law and brothers to do the dance they did at the wedding. I had no idea they could dance like that." Siobhan loved Michael Jackson, and her husband, along with Siobhan and Morgan's brothers, did a dance presentation at their wedding reception from "Smooth Criminal."

"I wish I could have seen it."

"Oh, I recorded it," she said, going over to retrieve her cell from her purse. She found the video and handed Brooke the phone.

"Wow, I didn't know your brothers could move like this. Your brother-in-law is one good-looking man."

"Justin is a great guy and perfect for my sister."

Brooke handed the phone back. "Do you think they'd be willing to do a special presentation for us?"

Morgan shrugged. "I don't know, but I'll ask. We'll be cutting it kind of close for Malcolm, though. Preseason starts at the end of the month. Since the show is scheduled the weekend before, he might be able to do it." They discussed the logistics of the added dances, as well as having a couple of Brooke's friends who were dancers to help with the choreography.

"I still want to do the instructor feature again, and this time, Morgan Gray, you will be dancing. You can do tap, jazz, hip-hop or whatever, but you will be dancing."

Morgan groaned. "Come on, Brooke. I haven't been on a stage in years," she protested.

Brooke rose gracefully to her feet. "No time like the present to get back out there. You're good, Morgan. I've watched you practice, and you haven't lost your edge. It's time the world knows that the dance teacher can *dance*. I've already reserved the hotel for the after-party. It's going to be fabulous. Oh, and this year, I want the dress rehearsal to be a private performance for the families of our students," she added.

"That's fine." Morgan was still a little unsure of being onstage again, but truthfully, she missed the excitement of performing for an audience. However, between getting her students prepared, working on the lawsuit and now writing Omar's contract, she didn't see how she would manage to learn a routine in less than a month's time.

Three nights later, Morgan sat at her kitchen table, reading over the contract she'd drawn up for Omar one last time to make sure she had included everything from general principles to the term of the contract. Compensation would be the standard 3 percent, but the only thing she needed to clarify was whether he wanted her for any other services, such as endorsements, or just the football deal. She reached for the card that had been included in the envelope of information and stared at the number. She took a glimpse at the microwave clock and noted it was past ten.

"You can do this, Morgan. It's what you've always wanted." Before she could talk herself out of calling, she took a deep breath and punched in the number on her cell.

"Hello," came the warm baritone.

Why does everything about this man have to be so sexy, including his voice? "Hey, Drummond. It's Morgan. I wanted to see when you're available to go over the contract."

"What are you doing tomorrow night?"

"I have something until eight, but I'm free afterward. I can meet you somewhere."

"I'd rather not meet in public."

Morgan's pulse skipped. She was counting on the buffer that a public place would provide. "I'm sure we could arrange a private room or something."

"That won't work," Omar insisted. "We can meet at my house, and I'll explain why when you get here."

His house? This had disaster written all over it. If they couldn't contain themselves at her brother's house, where almost two dozen people were, how would they manage with the two of them alone?

"I need you to trust me on this, Morgan. You've already set the rules, and I said I'd abide by them," he added softly.

"Okay." She wrote down the address he rattled off. "I should get there around nine."

"Thank you."

"You're welcome." Morgan disconnected and banged the phone softly against her forehead. "What am I getting myself into?" True, she had set the rules, but it would take everything within her not to break them.

The next evening, butterflies danced in Morgan's belly

as she rang Omar's doorbell. A measure of excitement filled her with the prospect of being able to break into the world of sports management. At the same time, she couldn't help but wonder what her family would think. Her dad had been dropping hints about her taking a more prominent role in the company, but so far she'd been able to dodge the questions. She hadn't told anyone aside from Brooke and Malcolm what she was doing.

Morgan turned to look at the beautifully manicured lawn and gave herself a pep talk about keeping her attraction under control. She whirled around at the sound of the door opening. She worked hard to keep her eyes on his face. Even wearing a T-shirt and basketball shorts, the man was temptation personified.

"Hey. Come on in." Omar waved her inside.

"I took the back roads and managed to avoid some traffic, so I'm a little early. I hope that's not a problem."

"Not at all. I'm fixing something to eat. Are you hungry?"

She followed him through the foyer with marble flooring and an elegantly furnished living room to a large modern kitchen. The smells wafting from the oven hit her nose, and immediately her stomach growled. She had eaten only a small salad before her dance class and was starving.

He laughed. "I'll take that as a yes."

Morgan smiled. "I didn't have time to go home for dinner. Whatever you're cooking smells great."

"Well, when your parents own a restaurant, everybody learns to cook."

"I didn't know your parents owned a restaurant or that you could cook. Somehow that didn't come up with the jock and playboy descriptions I've read."

He shifted his gaze from the pot he was stirring to her. "There's a lot about me you don't know. And don't believe everything you read."

Morgan felt properly chastised, because she had believed much of what had been printed in the newspapers about him. "Fair enough. What are you cooking?"

Omar took a spoon from a drawer, scooped a portion of what she realized was chili from the pot and handed it to her. "Taste and tell me what you think."

She blew on it a couple of times to cool it, then tentatively slid the spoon into her mouth. The thick, spicy concoction made her taste buds want to dance. "This is so good. Your parents taught you well." He removed a pan of cornbread from the oven and placed it on a trivet. "That's from a box, right?"

"Of course not," he said with mock offense. "My mother would have my head if I made cornbread from a box. Besides, this tastes much better." He cut a few pieces, placed them on a plate and handed it to Morgan. "Can you take this to the table?"

"Sure." The perfectly browned bread made her mouth water.

"Have a seat." He took two bowls out of the cabinet, filled them and took them to the kitchen table. "I made a pitcher of iced tea. I noticed that's all you drank last weekend."

"Great." Had he been paying that much attention to her? Maybe she needed to reassess her original assumptions about him.

Omar sat across the table, concentrating on his food and trying to ignore Morgan's seductive fragrance and how good she looked in those snug jeans. He was still a little put out by her judging him as a womanizer. He didn't claim to be a saint, and he'd dated his fair share of women, but he'd never cheated on one or bed-hopped as the media alleged.

"You're a really great cook, and this cornbread is to die for," Morgan said.

"Thanks. You can take some home with you. I don't need to eat it all."

"Probably not, since preseason is coming up."

"Speaking of football, you said you wanted to go over the contract."

"I do, but I have a couple of questions first."

"You want to know why I insisted you come to my house." When she nodded, he said, "You know as well as I do how intrusive the public can be. If we were spotted together with papers in front of us, it would be all over the media before we finished dinner."

"True, but it wouldn't be unusual for a client to meet with his agent."

"Unless he hasn't formally cut ties with his current agent yet."

"What?" Morgan moved to stand. "I can't play these games."

Omar placed a staying hand on her arm. "Hear me out, Morgan." He waited until she sat. "I haven't said anything to Roland because I'm still waiting for more information."

"You think he's embezzled from more of your endorsements?"

He nodded grimly. "At least one or two more. I need to keep this between us until I can get all the pieces." Just the thought made his blood boil. He wanted nothing more than to wring the man's neck, but that would ruin Omar's future plans.

"Okay. Were you able to contact Jaedon Dupree?"

"I'll be meeting with him on Tuesday." He paused. "I can't tell you how much I appreciate you helping me out."

"Yeah, well, don't thank me yet. I've never done this before."

Omar smiled. "But I've seen you play and heard you yelling in the stands. You know this game well, so I'm not worried. We're going to be good together." He realized what he'd said as soon as the words left his mouth. Clearing his throat, he pointed at the folder on the table. "You said you had some questions." Morgan eyed him, wiped her hand on a napkin and pushed one folder in front of him. She spoke with the clarity and confidence of someone who had done this several times over, and he found himself even more impressed by her intelligence.

"The biggest question I have is contract services. We never discussed whether it would include endorsements, but I propose we focus first on getting you a good deal with the Cobras for the next few years, then decide the rest later."

"That sounds like a good idea." He was ready to jump in with both feet but appreciated her wisdom. He already had two endorsement deals, and Roland had been calling for the past two weeks, trying to pin Omar down to a time to meet with another company. Omar had been ignoring his messages. Many players were envious of Roland's tenacity when it came to securing product endorsements for his clients, and now Omar knew why. Chances were Omar wasn't the only one the man had stolen from.

"That covers everything. Do you have any questions for me?"

He had quite a few. Did she have a boyfriend? If not, would she go on a date with Omar? And when was she going to let him kiss her again? But none of those was appropriate, so he answered, "No." He penned his signature in all the right places on both copies, pushed the folder back toward her and waited while she did the same. She gave him a copy and stood. Omar followed suit. He wasn't ready for her to leave and tried to think of a reason to make her stay, but it was getting late.

"I'd better go."

He wrapped her some food to go and led her out to the front through the family room.

She stopped abruptly, and a huge smile blossomed on her face. "You have 'Madden'?"

He followed her gaze to the television, where the popular football video game was frozen on the screen. "You want to play?"

"Maybe some other time."

His insides smiled. That meant she would be coming back to his house. Outside, they stood next to her car, and he clenched his fists at his sides to keep from reaching up to push the hair out of her face and stroke a finger down her satiny cheek.

Morgan held up the bag. "So, um…thanks for the food. I'll call you on Sunday to set up another time for us to talk."

Omar nodded. "You're welcome." They stood there for several charged seconds before she slid in behind the wheel. "See you later." He closed the door quickly to keep from pulling her out and into his arms. He shook his head as her taillights disappeared. *There's no way I'm going to make it for the next month and a half without kissing her.*

Chapter 4

The next Monday morning, Morgan checked and double-checked to make sure she had all the files needed for her meeting with the Sandersons' attorney. Brandon, her father and Mr. Whitcomb, her father's best friend and a minor partner in the company, would be joining them. Mr. Whitcomb—whom they affectionately called Uncle Thad—and Morgan's father had served together in the military, where Mr. Whitcomb sustained a serious injury. Disappointed by the lack of services for his disabled friend, her dad and started designing accessibility products in their home garage. Now their in-home safety company was one of the largest in the country.

Walking to the outer office, she stopped at her assistant's desk. "Evelyn, can you make sure the coffee and tea is set up in the small conference room, please?"

Evelyn came to her feet in a huff. "Yes, Ms. Gray," she said with a sarcastic smile.

Morgan silently counted to ten. Something had to give with this woman, and soon.

Brandon was already in the conference room when she arrived. "Hey, big brother."

"Hey. Ready?"

"Yep. I just hope Mr. Porter keeps his smart-aleck comments to himself this time." Several minutes later, she went over to the table where Evelyn had set up the coffee service and made a cup of mint tea. Whenever she felt nervous or stressed, the tea always calmed her.

"Well, I'm sure with Dad, Uncle Thad and me here, he won't try it today."

"It shouldn't have to be this way in the first place."

"True, but you already knew the kind of opposition you'd face when you decided to become an attorney."

Before Morgan could reply, her father and Uncle Thad entered the conference room. "Morning, Dad, Uncle Thad."

"Morning, baby," her father said.

Uncle Thad rolled his wheelchair over to where Morgan sat and smiled. "Good morning, Morgan."

Moments later, Mr. Porter was escorted in by one of the assistants. The fifty-something-year-old attorney had a slight build, a few gray strands peppering his short, dark brown hair and still wore that self-righteous smile.

"Good morning, Mr. Porter," Morgan said and made introductions. "You've met Brandon already. There are coffee and tea on the table if you'd like to pour yourself a cup before we get started." She gestured to the table. Obviously the man hadn't expected her show of authority, if his expression was any indication. She smiled inwardly.

Mr. Porter got coffee and came back to the table. "Good to see you here this morning, Mr. Gray. I'm certain we'll be able to make some real progress this time."

Brandon slanted Morgan a look that said, *Is this guy for real?*

"As I told Ms. Gray at our initial meeting, and I'm sure you all will agree, it would be in the best interest of your company if we settled this matter out of court. I don't have to remind you of the injuries my client suffered and the long-term care she'll require. The stress is wearing on the Sandersons, and they're anxious to have this settled."

"With all due respect, Mr. Porter, we will make a decision once we review all the evidence," Morgan said. "I've left messages at your office three times requesting the defective shower rail and packaging and have yet to receive a return call. Since you're here, we can schedule a time right now. I'm free next Wednesday at nine or Friday at eleven, or the following Tuesday at three. These are also the available dates provided by the third-party company you suggested. I took the liberty of hiring them in anticipation of our meeting today. Which one works best for you?" She pulled up the calendar on her iPad. "Either of those dates works for me." Morgan glanced at Brandon.

"Works for me."

Both her father and uncle nodded their agreement.

Morgan shifted her attention back to the lawyer. "Mr. Porter?" She smiled. "You mentioned that your clients are anxious to have the matter settled, and we agree."

"Well, I... I need to check with my secretary first." He looked downright uncomfortable.

"By all means." She rose and slid the telephone in front of him. "We can wait."

Mr. Porter reluctantly picked up the receiver and made the call. "Wednesday at nine," he muttered after hanging up.

"Great. Once we inspect the rail and run some tests—"

Mr. Porter leaned forward. "Tests?"

"Yes. Your clients claim that the rail broke. We want to know why, as I'm sure you do."

"Ah, yes, yes. Well, if there's nothing else, I have another meeting. I'll see you on Wednesday."

"Dad, do you have anything you want to add?"

"No. I think you've covered everything. Thad?"

"I'm satisfied."

"As am I," Brandon said.

"Then we're adjourned," Morgan said, rising to her feet. She walked around the table and extended her hand. "Thank you for coming, Mr. Porter. I look forward to seeing you next Wednesday."

He stood and gave her hand a brief shake, then gathered up his papers and made a hasty exit.

Morgan closed the door behind him and turned back to the table. "Well?"

"I'm proud of the way you handled yourself, baby girl," her father said. "Excellent job. I think Mr. Porter will think twice before he underestimates you again."

Uncle Thad chuckled. "Nolan, I think you're right."

"Thanks," she said. After the two men left, she turned to Brandon. "I expected you to say more."

"I didn't need to. I enjoyed that little show. Girl, you grilled him with a smile. I'm proud of you."

"Thanks. The way he's trying to rush this through makes me think something isn't right with their story."

"I was thinking the same thing." Brandon pushed to his feet. "But I know you'll get to the bottom of it. Been meaning to ask how you like working for the company."

Morgan shrugged. "It's okay. I'm just not sure this is where I want to work long-term."

"But you're good at it. You're not still thinking about that whole sports agent thing, are you? If you are, you might want to get a few years of legal experience first."

She didn't comment. No way would she tell him about Omar or the fact that she'd taken and passed the certification test to become an agent earlier in the year.

"Look, I know you love football, and I'm not saying you couldn't make it as a sports agent. I just don't see a lot of male athletes taking you seriously, and I don't want you to get your feelings hurt."

"Well, we'll just wait and see. Right now I'm concentrating on this case. See you around." She gathered up her folders and walked out.

Later, Morgan sat at her desk checking Omar's stats and salary from the previous year. As a tight end, his salary cap was much lower than that of a wide receiver. But when one of the receivers was injured last season, Omar had stepped in and played the position so well, that he'd earned the nickname End Zone Drummond. His numbers were second only to those of the team's star receiver, Marcus Dupree. Colin Rush was still questionable for the first half of the upcoming season, which would leave the team weak on the left side. She smiled. She'd just found her negotiating point.

When she talked to Omar tomorrow evening, she would share her thoughts. Automatically her mind went back to the kiss she couldn't seem to forget. She shook her head. "No kisses. *Just* the contract, Morgan," she muttered under her breath. The headache she'd gone through with her pro basketball boyfriend should make it easy to keep things strictly business with Omar, especially since his reputation with women mirrored that of her cheating ex. So no matter how delicious she thought his kisses were, there would be no more.

Tuesday, Omar first had a meeting with the group of people who had been selected to assist him in opening a mental center for veterans and their families. With so little resources, the service was sorely needed. Nine people sat on the board—veterans, family members of veterans, a psychologist and medical doctor. By the time the meeting ended, he had been talked into serving as the keynote speaker for the upcoming fund-raiser this weekend to replace the original woman who needed to leave town to take care of her ailing mother.

Afterward Omar had to rush to get to his appointment with Jaedon Dupree. Once there, he took the elevator in the Wilshire District office building and exited on the fifth floor. He crossed the plush carpet to the receptionist desk and greeted the woman sitting there with a smile.

"Good afternoon. My name is Omar Drummond. I have an appointment with Jaedon Dupree for two-thirty."

She pushed a button, spoke through a headset and then

nodded. "Go through these doors, turn right and you'll see his assistant's desk at the end of the hallway."

"Thank you." Omar followed her instructions and was greeted by another young woman.

"Hello, Mr. Drummond. Mr. Dupree is finishing up with a call. Please have a seat and he'll be with you in just a minute."

He nodded and glanced down at her nameplate. "Thank you, Ms. Ford." He sat in one of the three chairs, picked up a food magazine and flipped through the pages. Omar made a mental note to stop by his brother's house later to check on him. Rashad had been working in their family's restaurant helping out with stock since his discharge from the Army, and Omar hadn't talked to him in almost two weeks.

"Mr. Drummond?"

His head came up.

"Mr. Dupree will see you now."

Omar tossed the magazine on the table, stood and followed her into a large office.

"Thank you, Yvonne." Jaedon Dupree bore a startling resemblance to his brother, Marcus, and matched Omar in height and size. He came around his desk and extended his hand. "End Zone Drummond. Good to see you again, man."

He grinned. "Same here."

Jaedon gestured to a leather chair. "Have a seat."

He lowered himself into the offered chair. "Thanks for seeing me on such short notice. I know you're busy."

"No problem. What's going on?"

Omar handed Jaedon the large envelope. "I need you to represent me in a lawsuit against my agent."

Jaedon narrowed his eyes and pulled out the stack of papers. "Your agent is Roland Foster, right?"

He nodded.

"These are the same contract."

"Until you get to the flagged pages." He leaned over and pointed. "This is the copy Roland gave me to sign, and this one," he said, indicating the other copy, "is the original one from the watch company."

"So he siphoned seventy-five thousand off the top, plus his percentage."

"Exactly. He did the same thing with two others of my endorsements. Another seventy-five off the body wash one and half a mil from the sports drink." When Omar first saw that seventy-five-thousand-dollar difference, it had taken every ounce of his control not to storm over to Roland's house and beat the man to a pulp. He'd found out about the alteration when he ran into one of the executives he had met with at the watch company. The man congratulated him on the multimillion dollar contract with a number considerably higher than Omar remembered signing. And when asked, had provided Omar with another copy of the original contract.

Jaedon shook his head. "When's your contract up?"

"A month and a half. But he won't be negotiating it."

"I haven't seen anything in the news about you firing him, and I know that would've made the news."

"Because I haven't yet. I wanted to talk to you first and see if you would take the case."

"I will. Do you need some references for another agent? I know a few reputable guys."

"No. I already have one. Morgan Gray."

"I've never heard of him."

Omar chuckled. "That's because he's a *she* and I'm her first client. She's Malcolm Gray's twin sister."

Recognition dawned. "The attorney working for their family's company?"

"Yes."

Jaedon frowned. "Isn't she kind of young? If I remember correctly, she's only two or three years out of law school."

"She is. But she knows football, and I don't want to deal with anyone connected to league politics. My first agent negotiated a one-year deal so bad I probably could have made more working in a fast-food restaurant. After that, when my ex-girlfriend forged my name on some reality TV deal she was trying to get, my second agent was nowhere to be found. He didn't back my claims of not knowing anything about the deal and tried to get me to consider doing the show. My guess, it was because of the dollar amount he figured he'd get. And now Roland." He shook his head. "I'm done."

"I didn't know all that. Do you think Morgan will be able to handle herself with team management?"

"I admit that it has crossed my mind, but I'm not too concerned about it." In fact, that was the least of Omar's worries.

"But…" When Omar didn't respond, a slow grin made its way over Jaedon's face. "But you're attracted to her."

"Yeah."

"It might not be—"

Omar held up a hand. "She's already set the ground rules."

He laughed. "Which means it's not one-sided. I've met Morgan. She's a beautiful woman. Let me know how that works out for you."

"Sounds like you're in the same boat. Someone in your office?"

"No. The personal chef I just hired. Anyway, when are you going to call Roland?"

"As soon as I leave here."

"Good. I'll get the ball rolling. I've met Roland, and I don't think he's going to take this lying down. Are you prepared for media?"

"I am." In reality it was the last thing he wanted, especially with the fund-raiser coming up this weekend. But he'd deal with it. He stood. "Thanks for everything, Jaedon."

Jaedon followed suit. "No problem. I'll let you know when he's been served so you can be prepared."

"I'd appreciate it."

"By the way, Marcus told me about the mental health center you're trying to open. It's a good thing. I'll be there on Saturday."

"I'll be glad for the support." The two men shook hands, and Omar headed back down to the garage where his car was parked. He slid behind the wheel, pulled out his cell and called Roland. Just the mere thought of the man spiked Omar's anger all over again. But the sooner he ended the relationship, the better he'd be, mentally and financially.

"I've been trying to call you for the past two and a half weeks," Roland started in before Omar could say a word. "We need to jump on this deal with Apple. I can't keep putting them off."

He knew that deal would most likely net a lucrative contract, but Roland wouldn't be handling it. If Apple was serious and things worked out with Morgan, maybe he'd ask her to negotiate the contract. He felt certain she would be honest in her dealings.

"So I need you to get over here and—"

"Roland," Omar interrupted. "I won't be coming by your office tonight or ever. We're done."

There was a slight pause, then Roland said, "What the hell do you mean, we're done? After all I've done for you. You would've never been able to negotiate a deal to become one of the highest paid tight ends had it not been for me. You *need* me, Drummond."

"Are you sure it's not the other way around?"

The agent went silent for a moment. "Exactly what are you implying?"

"I'm not implying anything. I'm opting out of my contract."

"You can't do that to me," he yelled.

"Sure I can. Remember that clause that says either of us can terminate the contract if the other doesn't live up to the agreement? You haven't, so I'm exercising that option. You'll be hearing from my attorney." Roland's curses filled Omar's ear as Omar ended the call. He blew out a long breath and felt a weight being lifted off his chest. He smiled, started the engine and drove across town to his brother and sister-in-law's house.

He was relieved to see his brother's truck parked in the driveway. Every so often something would trigger some sort of flashback for Rashad and he'd disappear for hours, sometimes days. And when he returned, looked as if he'd been sleeping on the streets. Six months ago, after much discussion, Rashad had allowed Omar to buy him a small trailer where he could go when he needed time alone. So far it had worked out and made it easier on his wife and children, as well as the rest of their family.

"Uncle Omar!"

His twelve-year-old niece, Brianna, flew off the porch and across the grass before Omar could close the car door. It seemed like she had added another inch or two to her slender frame since he'd seen her last and, with her smooth mocha skin, dark eyes and wide smile, was a mini replica of her beautiful mother. She launched herself at him as soon as he rounded the fender, and he scooped her up and swung her around. Setting her gently on her feet, he placed a kiss on her temple. "How's my favorite niece?" he asked with a grin.

"I'm your *only* niece," she answered with a playful roll of her eyes. "I'm good."

"You enjoying your summer break?" he asked as they strolled up the walk.

"Yes and no."

"What's the problem?"

"There's nothing to do…except the stupid report Mom makes us write. I want to take a dance class, but she said I'd have to wait awhile."

"Well, that report is important." His librarian sister-in-law made his niece and nephew write a Black history report every summer, saying they couldn't know where they were going unless they knew where they'd been. "As far as the dance class, you keep doing what you're supposed to and I'm sure your mom will let you take one." Omar held open the screen door.

Brianna pouted and mumbled, "I guess."

He shook his head and followed her into the house. His ten-year-old nephew, Rashad Jr., was in his usual spot in front of the television, playing some video game. Omar playfully rubbed his head. "What's up, little man?"

"Hey, Uncle O," Rashad Jr. said without taking his eyes off the screen.

"Where's your mom?" he asked Brianna.

"In the kitchen," she called over her shoulder and veered off down a hallway.

He continued to the kitchen. "Hey, Serena."

"Omar," she said, drying her hands on a dish towel and coming over to hug him. "How are you?"

"Good. What about you?" He studied her pained expression.

"Yesterday, not so great. But today is better."

He nodded, knowing she was talking about his brother. "Anything you need me to do?"

"No. But you're welcome to stay for dinner if you want. Rashad asked for fried chicken, so that's what I'm making."

"You know I never turn down your fried chicken. Where is he?"

"Outside in the backyard."

Omar went out the sliding glass door off the kitchen and spotted his brother sitting on the grass beneath a large shade tree.

"Hey, little brother," Rashad called.

"Hey."

Rashad smiled. "Serena call you because I had a bad day yesterday?"

"No. I didn't know you had one. How's today?"

He shrugged. "Better, I guess."

"What happened yesterday?"

"Had one of those stupid shrink sessions. The man acted like he had somewhere he needed to be. Kept checking his watch every five minutes, then asked if we could call it a day." He slanted Omar a glance. "Fifteen minutes into the session. Made me upset. I'm not going back. Tired of being treated like I'm nobody."

Omar sighed inwardly. This was the second psychiatrist Rashad had seen. It had taken several months for him to receive the service. The first one only wanted to prescribe medication, to which his brother was adamantly opposed, and the current one had a habit of canceling or shortening appointments. It was even more reason why he wanted to open the center. He started to speak and his cell rang. Not wanting to interrupt his brother now that he was opening up, he let it ring.

"You going to answer that?"

"I can call whoever it is back later."

Rashad shook his head. "Answer your phone, Mr. Psychologist. This isn't a counseling session."

Omar chuckled and dug the cell out of his pocket. He went still upon seeing Morgan's name on the display. "Hey, Morgan."

"Hi, Drummond. Is this a good time to talk?"

"What's up?"

"I just wanted to see how your meeting with Jaedon Dupree went."

"It went well. Can I call you later? I'm talking to my brother."

"Of course. Why didn't you say so in the first place?"

"Your call is important."

"Drummond, I thought we—"

"Relax, Morgan. I just meant as far as our business is concerned."

"Oh. Sorry," she mumbled. "I'll be home around nine, if that's not too late for you."

Omar smiled. *Back to business.* "No. I'll call you around nine-thirty." Rashad was staring at him with a silly grin on his face when Omar hung up. "What?"

"Baby brother's got a new girl. It's been a while."

This was the brother he remembered and grew up with. At thirty-four and six years Omar's senior, Rashad had taught him everything he knew about women. Omar had idolized his big brother and tried to emulate his every move, from his walk and the way he talked to his smooth reputation when it came to the ladies. "I don't have a new girl. Just a new agent."

"This I have got to hear."

They shared a smile, and Omar filled him in on what had led up to him firing Roland and hiring Morgan.

Later, after arriving home, he decided to shower first. Then he'd call Morgan to let her know about his conversation with Jaedon and invite her to be his date for the fundraiser. Now that he'd fired Roland, he was free to be seen with her in public and wanted to introduce her as his new agent. He only hoped he'd be able to keep his hands off her.

Chapter 5

Morgan added the finishing touches to her makeup Saturday evening and surveyed her look. The navy off-the-shoulder floor-length gown dipped modestly in the front and had a front slit to the knee. Nothing too revealing. She didn't want to give Omar or anyone else the impression that their relationship was anything but business. The fluttering increased in her stomach. Ever since Omar had asked her to attend a benefit dinner with him—their first public appearance together—her nerves had been on edge. Though this was supposed to be business, somehow it felt like a real date. What would people think? And what would her family say? Outside Malcolm, she hadn't gotten up the courage to tell the rest of them. Siobhan was due back to work next week, so she'd talk to her.

Her mind went back to the benefit. Omar had mentioned it being held for a mental health center, but he hadn't been specific about the details. Morgan's curiosity was piqued, and she wished she knew more. The intercom sounded and her heart started racing.

"Yes?"

"Omar," came the warm baritone.

She buzzed him in and drew in a deep, calming breath before opening the door. Her breath caught at the sight of him looking as if he'd just left a photo shoot for *GQ* magazine.

"So…can I come in?" Omar asked with a knowing grin.

Morgan wanted to kick herself. No way would he take her seriously about keeping things strictly professional if she stared at him like a starstruck groupie every time she saw him. "Of course." She stepped back, waved him in and walked over to the end table where she'd left her purse.

"You look stunning." His gaze made a slow tour down her body and an even slower one back up. Their eyes met. "Stunning."

What have I gotten myself into? Morgan didn't see how she would be able to resist him for the next few weeks. She didn't know if she'd make it through tonight. "Thanks. You clean up pretty well yourself." Instead of all black, he had opted for a white jacket. His tuxedo caressed his tall, lean frame, and she had visions of undoing—

Abruptly halting her erotic fantasy, she chastised herself again. She had never lost her mind over a man before and had no intentions of starting now. "I'm ready." Morgan slung the thin strap of her silver evening bag over her shoulder and started for the door. Omar caught her hand. The contact sent an electric current up her arm.

"Morgan, I just want you to know how much I appreciate you taking a chance on me." He bent and placed a soft kiss on her cheek.

She ignored the potency of his cologne and the sensations flowing through her that his kiss invoked and said, "You're welcome. I could say the same for you." They shared a smile. The intensity of his stare made her pulse skip, and she turned away. "We don't want to be late." Morgan locked the door behind them and hurried down the walk. He led her to a newer-model silver BMW and held the door open. She slid in and leaned back against the butter-soft leather.

Omar stepped in on the driver's side and got them underway. "I've never seen your hair straight like this. I didn't know it was that long. I like it."

"Thank you." She unconsciously brought a hand up and smoothed down the sleek, straight strands. Most times she left it curly. "It started as a bet between Malcolm and me two years ago to see who could grow their hair the longest—mine straight and his with locs." Malcolm's locs had reached his shoulder blades before he trimmed them to just below his neck. Morgan had continued to let hers grow, and her hair now reached the middle of her back.

"I guess you won, huh?"

"Yes. But, I've been thinking about cutting it."

"Don't do that," he said quickly. Omar's eyes left the road briefly and found hers. "It's beautiful."

Although they shouldn't have, his words pleased her. He smiled over at her, and she felt the heat rising between them. To distract herself she asked, "So tell me about the center. How long has it been open?"

"They just broke ground, and it's projected to open next March."

"Do you know the people who will run it, or are you just going to support it?"

"Both."

She waited for him to elaborate, but he said nothing else. Silence slipped between them. A moment later, soft music filled the car's interior.

"Is there too much air on you? I tend to run hot and I'm usually the only one in the car, so I forget to turn it down."

Morgan was running a little hot herself, and it had nothing to do with the ninety-degree July weather. "It's fine."

"How are you feeling about tonight?"

Her brows knit together. "What do you mean?"

"Dealing with the questions and comments."

"I'll be fine. I'm sure there will be at least one person who has something negative to say, but as a lawyer, I deal with it all the time. I have two strikes against me—I'm a woman and I'm only twenty-seven."

"Well, I'd better not hear one disrespectful comment."

She chuckled. "Before you go all caveman, remember,

I'm *your* agent. It's my job to protect you, not the other way around. Save that for your girlfriends."

"I don't have any *girlfriends*. I haven't dated anyone seriously in almost four years."

Her head snapped around. "What about all the pictures that have been popping up of you with one woman or the other? And the media—"

"We've already been down this road," Omar said with a slight edge. "Don't believe everything the media says." He sighed heavily. "Look, Morgan, I'm not saying I've lived my life as a saint. I've made my share of mistakes just like everybody else, but that was when I was younger." He pulled into the valet lane at the hotel, put the car in Park and turned to face her. "When you open yourself up to someone and find out that she only wants to use you, it makes you grow up fast. And you're not too eager to do it all over again."

It had never occurred to her that he might have had his heart broken in the past. "I'm sorry. As an attorney, I should know better than to judge without all the facts." Morgan stuck out her hand. "No more judging. Deal?"

He smiled and reached for her hand. "Deal."

He lifted her hand to his lips, and she snatched it away. "What do you think you're doing? No. Kisses."

"That was just a…" He trailed off at her look.

"Did you ever kiss your other agents?"

Omar lifted a brow. "My other agents didn't look like you."

Morgan skewered him with a glare.

He raised his hands in mock surrender. "Okay, okay. You're right." He glanced over his shoulder and saw the valet standing outside the door. "I guess we should get out. Ready to face the masses?"

She smiled. "Let's do it."

Shaking his head, Omar got out and came around to her side. "Is helping you out of the car allowed?"

She placed her hand in his. "Ha-ha, you got jokes now."

"Hey, I'm just trying to keep my agent from dropping me before I get to the bargaining table."

She cut him a look and rolled her eyes. "Let's go, Drummond."

He chuckled and escorted her inside.

As soon as they entered the ballroom, several pairs of eyes swung their way, all filled with surprise. The butterflies that had previously calmed returned in full force. "Oo-kay. I guess it's showtime."

"Yep."

Before they could take a step, a man headed toward them with a wide smile.

"Long time no see, Drummond," the man said, shaking Omar's hand. Although he had spoken to Omar, his eyes were locked on Morgan.

"It has been a while. Morgan, this is Garrett Butler, an old college classmate. Garrett, my agent, Morgan Gray."

Morgan bit back a smile at the man's stunned gaze. "It's nice to meet you."

"Same here." Garrett glanced back at Omar. "Didn't hear you'd changed agents."

"It just happened recently," Omar replied mildly.

"Well, congratulations and good luck in the upcoming season. Ms. Gray, it was a pleasure." He nodded her way and departed.

"That was easy," Morgan murmured. "I hope it's a sign of things to come."

"Yes, let's hope. Come on. I want to introduce you to a few people, and then we'll get our seats."

"Okay." After the first one or two people, the names and faces started to blur. But so far, no one had been rude. He stopped at a table in the front, dead center, and pulled out a chair for her. "Do we need to sit so close?" She had no desire to have her every move scrutinized the entire evening.

"It'll be fine." He lowered himself into the chair beside her.

A man approached the table. "Omar. I'm glad you're here. Can I talk to you for a minute?"

"Sure. Morgan, this is a good friend of mine, Bryson Harper. He's the board's chairman. Bryce, my agent, Morgan Gray."

Bryson grinned. "Nice to meet you, Ms. Gray. About time he showed up with somebody who looks better than the last three agents he's had. You won't get a better client than this one," he said, clapping Omar on the shoulder.

A smile lit Morgan's face, and she laughed. "Thank you."

"Mind if I borrow Omar?"

"Not at all."

"Be back in a minute," Omar told her.

Morgan watched Omar's fluid gait as he walked away. Alone, she took the opportunity to check out the guests. She saw city dignitaries, football players and even a few sports agents in the sea of people mingling. She caught a glimpse of Jaedon Dupree standing in a small group and smiled inwardly at a woman trying to insert herself into the conversation. Not that Morgan could blame her. Morgan had met Jaedon at a conference where he was one of several presenters. With his towering height, mesmerizing voice and green eyes, he'd held the attention of every female lawyer in the building.

Her brother waved from across the room and started in her direction. Then Malcolm bent and kissed her cheek. "Hey, sis. I didn't know you were going to be here tonight."

"We decided to make the announcement on our terms instead of waiting for the media to spin it."

"It's a good strategy. And the other parts?"

"Other parts of what?"

"The relationship."

"There is no relationship. It's strictly business."

A smile played around his lips. "If you say so. Have you told the family yet?"

"Not yet," she said with a heavy sigh.

"You do realize your face is going to be all over the news after tonight. Better for them to hear it from you."

"I know. Maybe I'll do it at dinner tomorrow." The entire family got together at least monthly for Sunday dinner. "Daddy's probably going to have a fit. And Brandon just told me this week that I should focus on being a lawyer right now."

He squeezed her shoulder. "Well, you know I got your back."

"Thanks, Mal."

Omar returned, and he and Malcolm shared a one-arm hug. "What's up, man?"

"I see you have a new agent," Malcolm said. "I hope it works out."

Staring down at Morgan, he said, "I'm counting on it."

Malcolm chuckled, and Morgan cut him a quick look.

"Looks like they're about to serve dinner. I'll see you guys later."

Over dinner, conversation flowed around the table. Morgan learned that the center's focus would be to provide services for veterans. She thought that was a great idea and made a mental note to mention it to her father. As veterans, he and Uncle Thad would more than likely want to pledge their support. After dinner, Bryson stepped up to the microphone and thanked everyone for attending. He provided detailed information on the center's goals and what they needed in the way of funding.

"I'd like to take credit for this dynamic project, but I can't," Bryson continued. "That honor belongs to our key-

note speaker and the center's founder, Omar Drummond."
Applause sounded throughout the ballroom.

Morgan gasped and swung her surprised gaze to Omar.
"You're the... Why didn't you tell me?" she whispered.

Omar shrugged, stood and made his way to the podium.
"Thanks, Bryce. And thank you all for coming."

He turned his serious gaze toward the audience, and
Morgan was held spellbound as he spoke about the limited and often difficult-to-access services for the country's
veterans. Omar then shared how his best friend, suffering from PTSD, committed suicide six months after being
discharged from the Army. Tears filled her eyes while she
listened to him talk about his older brother suffering from
the same disease and its effects on his wife and children.

Omar finished by saying, "Our servicemen and servicewomen have given everything, including their lives, to protect our freedom. It's about time we returned the favor."

The room erupted in applause, and Morgan was on her
feet with everyone else. When he came back to the table,
it was all she could do not to throw her arms around his
neck and kiss him. She settled for a gentle pat on his arm.
She leaned toward him. "You were absolutely amazing."

"That means a lot coming from you, Morgan. Thanks."

They were only a breath apart. If either of them
moved... Luckily someone came over and claimed Omar's
attention. Morgan reached for her glass of water and took
a big gulp. Many more people came over to congratulate
him, and he introduced Morgan as he had all evening.

A few minutes later, the music started and people took
to the dance floor. She nodded in time to the beat and
smiled at a few people who were really letting loose. She
turned back and found Omar staring at her with an intensity that made her heart rate speed up.

"Stop looking at me like that. You're going to make it
hard for people to believe I'm just your agent."

"Looking at you like what?"

"Like I'm your favorite dessert and you can't wait to gobble me up."

"You just might be," he murmured.

Morgan blinked.

He picked up his water goblet and took a sip. "And for the record, I never *gobble* up my dessert. I take my time, one spoonful at a time, and savor every delectable morsel. A great dessert should never be rushed."

To the casual observer, they might have been discussing the weather. His features remained neutral, but his words were hot enough to melt a heavy-gauge steel goalpost. Morgan usually had a comeback for everything, but this man had left her breathless…and speechless. "Um… I need to go to the bathroom. I'll be right back." She nearly jumped from her chair, and he smoothly came to his feet to help her up. Their bodies touched and she stifled a moan. Pretending to be impervious to his touch, she smiled and made her way to the nearest exit. Of all the football players in the league, why did her first shot at her dream have to be with the one man who affected her like no other?

Chapter 6

Omar drained the water in his glass and refilled it from one of the pitchers that had been placed on the table. He had promised himself that he was going to keep his desire for Morgan under wraps. It wasn't a good look, especially for someone who'd basically told her he wasn't eager to get his heart broken again. And it didn't help that nearly every man in attendance couldn't take his eyes off her. Each time he introduced her and somebody held her hand longer than politeness dictated or lingered over her shapely body, Omar had been tempted to punch the man.

But from the moment she opened the door to him, he'd been fighting a losing battle. And that dessert comment only heightened the growing passion between them. Omar wanted to taste and savor every inch of her. A vision of her body bared for his pleasure made him instantly hard. He groaned inwardly, picked up the glass and drained its contents. He tried to focus on something, anything that would extinguish the fire in his groin.

He turned when a hand touched his shoulder, and he smiled. Omar came to his feet swiftly and engulfed Serena in a hug. "I didn't know you were here."

Serena reached up to touch his face. "You know I had to come and support you. Rashad told me to tell you how proud he is of you. And so am I."

"Thanks, sis," he said around the lump in his throat.

She smiled. "Rashad also said that when you get your center up and running, maybe he'd give it a try."

"Really? That's a huge step." It was the first time his brother had ever voluntarily suggested getting help.

Tears shimmered in her eyes. "Yes, it is."

Omar glanced up in time to see Morgan crossing the floor.

Serena followed his gaze. "She's beautiful. New girl-friend?"

"No. My new agent."

A laugh escaped her mouth.

"What's so funny?"

"You. She might be your agent, but that's not all she'll be."

By this time, Morgan had reached them.

Not waiting for Omar to make introductions, Serena said, "Hi, I'm Serena Drummond, Omar's sister-in-law. I understand you're Omar's new agent."

"Morgan Gray. It's nice to meet you, Serena. And, yes, I'm his agent."

Serena divided her gaze between Omar and Morgan and smiled. "Whatever you two say. Morgan, it was great to meet you." She turned to Omar. "I need to get back home. Congratulations, baby brother."

"Thanks for coming. Tell Bri and RJ I'll be by to take them to lunch sometime next week."

"Lord, they're going to be so excited. You've got them so spoiled."

Omar laughed. "Hey, that's what uncles do."

Serena shook her head. "Bye, boy."

After she left, Morgan said, "She seems nice."

"She's an angel."

"I didn't know you had a brother."

"Remember when you came to my house? I told you there's a lot you don't know about me."

"Yeah. I'm finding that out."

"So, it seems we got through the evening pretty well."

"Aside from a couple of snippy comments by those two football players."

"I wouldn't worry about them. Once you get my contract squared away, I have a feeling every player around is going to be beating down your door. And they're going to be sorry they doubted you."

Morgan laughed. "That's right."

Omar joined in her laughter. In his peripheral vision he spotted Roland. His smile faded and he muttered a curse.

She frowned. "What's wrong?"

"Roland just walked in the door and he doesn't look happy."

"And he's coming this way."

As Morgan stated, Roland made a beeline for them.

Roland stopped in front of Omar and waved some papers in his face. "Who the hell do you think you are? You can't sue me."

Omar's jaw tightened. "Roland, this is not the time or the place."

"The time and place are wherever I damn well please. You won't get away with this. When I get through with you, you won't be able to get a contract playing Little League." He turned his hostile gaze on Morgan and chuckled bitterly. "And this is the bitch you replaced me with."

Omar took a step. "You—" The blistering look Morgan turned on Omar rendered him instantly silent.

Morgan fixed her cold, hard stare on Roland and spoke just loud enough for him to hear. "Mr. Foster, Mr. Drummond is now *my* client, and anything you have to say to him will go through *me*. You do realize that you just threatened my client in a room full of people. Let me make one thing clear. If I see or hear one libelous or slanderous statement, I will have you in front of a judge so fast you won't have time to say *bitch*! Now, is there anything else?"

Roland looked like he was about to explode, but he didn't say anything. Giving them one last glare, he stormed off.

For several seconds, Omar didn't move or breathe.

The frost in her voice had him scared to even think about opening his mouth. It was the most impressive thing he'd ever seen, and his respect for her went up another notch. "Damn, girl," he whispered in awe. When he'd first approached her about being his agent, Omar admittedly had some reservations about how she would fare in this hard-nosed business. But after witnessing how she had sliced Roland up into little pieces without ever raising her voice, he realized his concerns had been unwarranted.

"Are you okay?"

"I was going to ask you the same thing."

She gave him a faint smile. "I'm fine. I just hope Mr. Foster takes me at my word."

"So do I." He made a mental note to talk to Jaedon before leaving. He couldn't afford to have any negative press impacting the center. Or his new agent. Contrary to her statement about it being her job to protect him, he had every intention of protecting her, whether she liked it or not.

Morgan was still simmering inside from Roland Foster's audacity. She'd seen photos of him in the papers, but up close the short afro toupee he sported looked even worse. He had the stocky build of a boxer, but any muscles he might have had were long gone. The man had to be out of his mind to cause a scene and publicly threaten Omar. And when he'd called her that name…it had taken every fiber of her being not to knock that word right out of his mouth. But had she appeared to be in trouble for one instant, Malcolm would have come charging over. Between him and Omar, and the rest of her brothers once they got wind of it, it would have caused a scandal to rival the O. J. Simpson trial. Even as she stood talking with Bryson and a woman on the center's board, Malcolm kept one eye on her from his position across the room. She would be willing to bet any amount of money that he'd be calling or stopping by her condo tonight to get the details. The woman's voice pulled her back into the conversation.

"How long have you been a sports agent, Ms. Gray?"

"Mr. Drummond is my first client. I currently work as an attorney in my family's company."

"Impressive. On behalf of women everywhere, I applaud you. It's about time we bring a little diversity to the sports agency world."

"And you got the cream of the crop with your first client," Bryson said.

"I appreciate the vote of confidence." In her book, Omar was the cream of the crop in more ways than one.

A lull in the conversation gave Morgan a chance to take her leave. "If you'll excuse me, I see my client heading for the exit. It's been a pleasure meeting you. Good luck with the center." They shook hands, and she made her way toward Omar.

Omar smiled as she approached. "Are you ready?" she asked.

"Whenever you are." He gestured her forward.

Jaedon was leaving at the same time. "Hello, Morgan. It's been a while."

"It has. Congratulations on opening your firm," she said.

"Thanks. Congratulations to you, too. If you have any questions or if you need anything, let me know."

Morgan smiled. Coming from any other man, she might have perceived it as a put-down, but she knew he hadn't meant it that way. "I'll do that."

"I told him about what Roland did just now," Omar informed her.

Jaedon's lips settled in a grim line. "He's always been arrogant, but I never thought he was stupid. I have a private investigator friend of mine checking to see what else Roland is involved in. Let me know if he says anything else."

"I already let him know what would happen if he pulled another stunt like he did tonight," Morgan said, getting heated all over again.

Jaedon nodded. "Good enough, then. I'll let you two get out of here."

After leaving the hotel, they rode the first few minutes in silence. Finally Morgan asked, "Why didn't you tell me about your role in the center?"

"I don't know. You seemed to have an opinion of me already, and I thought I'd let my actions do the talking. I guess I wanted you to understand that there's more to me than what the media puts out."

"I see." Once again, he'd left her speechless. Not one media outlet had reported on all the good he was doing. Her emotions rose as she remembered how he had shared experiences about his friend and his brother.

"Actually, that was the other reason I decided to clean up my act—not like it was *that* bad in the first place." He slanted her an amused glance.

Morgan laughed softly. "Yeah, yeah. Anyway, I think what you're doing is fabulous and needed. My dad and Uncle Thad will definitely want to contribute since they're both veterans."

"We could use all the help we can get. I want to be able to offer a variety of services that don't revolve around medication—retreats with peers, ways to help them understand their new normal, family counseling—and address mind, body and soul."

His passion was infectious, and she found herself getting excited and wanting to do all she could to help. "You said 'I.' Do you plan to work at the center?"

"Eventually."

"Doing what?"

"As one of the clinical psychologists."

Morgan shifted in her seat to face him. "You'd need a doctorate in psychology in order to practice."

"I have a BS in psychology. I had planned to start applying to some doctorate programs before this mess with Roland. Now I'll probably wait until my contract is settled."

"Since we're talking about your contract, how many more years are you looking to play ball?"

"I'd like to get at least four, which is what management has offered. Roland was pushing me to go for six. Said I needed to get as much money up front as I could so I wouldn't be broke later." Omar snorted. "Probably more like so *he* could get as much money up front."

"Well, rest assured he won't get one more dime of your money. Ideally, Jaedon will be able to help you recover what he took. I assume you have a financial advisor."

"Yeah. I don't spend recklessly or waste my money on women and parties. I did offer to buy my parents a house early in my career, though." He chuckled.

"I take it by that laugh it didn't go too well."

"You take it right. My mother walked me through every inch of the twenty-five-hundred-square-foot, four-bedroom house that I grew up in, then planted her hands on her hips and asked me, 'Does it look like we need a new house?'"

Morgan burst out laughing. "Sounds like something my mother would say."

"Oh, she didn't stop there. What I didn't realize is that I'd opened up the floodgates to a lecture on financial and personal responsibility that lasted almost two hours." Omar shook his head. "I haven't asked her another question since, and that was five years ago."

Morgan laughed so hard she thought she was going to hurt herself.

He smiled. "I'm glad you think it's so funny."

"I'm sorry," she said, wiping tears of mirth from her eyes. "Well, did you listen?"

"Hell, yeah. And if you ever meet my mama, you'll see why. Once she actually had my dad drive her over to my house to make sure I hadn't lied about how many cars I own. For the record, I have only two—this one and my truck. Although I do have a motorcycle, too."

"You do?" she asked with excitement.

"Let me guess. You ride?"

"Just Malcolm's sometimes."

"I could take you riding if you want."

She shouldn't even have been contemplating going riding with this man, but she loved the way the wind felt on her face, the way the bike hugged the curves on the road. "We'll see." Silence crept between them and before she knew it, they were pulling into her complex. Morgan used the remote on her key ring to open the gate, and Omar parked in one of the visitors' spots. He walked her to the door and waited while she unlocked it.

Standing just inside, Morgan faced him. "So, I think things went pretty well tonight, aside from the one hiccup."

"I'm sorry about that."

She waved him off. "Don't worry about it. I told him what he needed to know. Will you be available next weekend to talk about the contract?"

"I had planned to go up to my cabin in Big Bear. I do it yearly to clear my mind before the new season."

"Oh," She understood. Malcolm usually did the same thing and had just returned from Belize a few weeks ago. "I guess it can wait. You need to have a clear head. We'll figure something out."

Omar nodded. "Okay. I guess I'd better get going."

She saw in his eyes that he didn't want to leave, and she could admit to herself that she didn't want him to go. He'd removed his jacket and tie and unbuttoned the first two buttons on his shirt. The man was sexy without even trying. He moved closer, then seemingly remembered the rules she'd set in place and stepped back.

"Good night, Morgan."

"Good night." She closed the door, leaned her head against it and released a deep sigh. She was glad one of them had thought about their agreement. Pushing away from the door, Morgan went to shower.

Afterward she scrubbed her face clean, made a cup of mint tea and curled up on the lounger in her bedroom with her notes from the lawsuit. She couldn't rid herself of the nagging feeling that she had missed something. She scanned the invoice to see if maybe one of the parts didn't get shipped, but everything was there. Morgan brought the mug to her lips, took a sip and groaned when she heard the doorbell. Setting the folder aside, she took her tea and went to open the door. "I'm fine," she said before she'd opened it all the way. "You didn't need to come all the way over here."

"How did you know it was me?" Malcolm asked.

Morgan rolled her eyes and left him standing there. "Seriously, Malcolm?" She sat on the sofa and tucked her feet beneath her. "You were watching me like you used to whenever you thought some boy was trying to talk to me."

He dropped down in a chair. "What did Roland say? And don't tell me it was nothing. The man was pissed and was loud enough for all of us two tables over to hear him threaten to ruin Drummond. Now, what did he say to you?"

She raised her eyes to the ceiling and whined, "Why do I have brothers? It was nothing I couldn't handle. If I'm going to be an agent, I can't have you running over here every time you think something has happened." The look on Malcolm's face said he couldn't have cared less about what she had said and didn't plan to leave until she gave him answers. "He called me a B."

"He *what*! When I get done with his ass—"

"Malcolm, you do *not* need to handle anything. I took care of it. I told him if I saw one thing in the media, I'd have him in front of a judge before he could call me that again."

He leaned back in the chair and chuckled.

"Satisfied? Now, let me deal with it."

Malcolm raised his palms in surrender. "You win."

"You didn't tell Brandon and Khalil, did you?"

"No, I wanted to talk to you first."

"Good. No sense in having all you nuts locked up behind some craziness. Since you're here, you want some tea?"

"No, thanks. I'm going home. How's the dance production coming?"

"It's good. I hope you guys will agree to do the dance. I'll give Justin a couple of days to recuperate from his honeymoon before I ask him."

"Are you going to invite Omar?"

"Hadn't planned on it. Attending a dance recital doesn't really fall under the scope of an agent-client relationship."

"No, but you know as well as I do there's more going on. You may not have acted on it yet, but you will." Malcolm stood, stretched and headed for the door.

Morgan followed. "I can't. This may be my only shot at becoming an agent, and I won't do anything to jeopardize that."

He turned back, placed his arm around her shoulder and kissed her temple. "So, you two *are* attracted to each other," he said with a chuckle. "Thanks for the confirmation."

She punched him in the chest and pushed him toward the door. "Go home."

"I'm going. And don't worry. I'll keep your secret." He smiled. "I always have."

"I know, and I love you."

"See you tomorrow. You want me to pick you up on the bike?"

"Yeah, come get me. I'll be ready around one-thirty. I told Mom I'd be there earlier than usual. With Siobhan gone, it'll just be her and I cooking."

"Okay."

Morgan kissed her brother on the cheek. "Night, Mal."

"Night, sis. Lock up."

"I will."

She was in big trouble. The mention of riding the motorcycle made her think of Omar's offer. She wanted to ride the bike…and the man.

Chapter 7

Morgan and Malcolm were the first to arrive at their parents' home Sunday afternoon. They found their mother in the kitchen standing over one of the sinks in the spacious kitchen. The large area had another sink at a center island, tons of counter and cabinet space, an oversize refrigerator and double oven.

"Well, if it isn't the daredevil twins," her mother teased. Though she had changed out of her dress, she still had on her earrings and makeup. As always, her cropped, layered salt-and-pepper hair didn't have a strand out of place, and her smooth light brown skin was virtually unlined. "How are you two?" Growing up, Malcolm had always been a risk-taker. Morgan had believed she could do anything he did and often mimicked her brother's antics.

"Good," Morgan said, and kissed her cheek.

Malcolm followed suit, then asked, "Where's Dad?"

"He was out back doing something."

"Well, I'll leave you two in here to whip up the goodies."

"Oh, you don't have to rush off, son," their mother said. "You can always stay and help."

Morgan chuckled at the panicked look on Malcolm's face.

He mumbled something unintelligible and made a hasty retreat.

"I guess that means he doesn't want to help," Morgan cracked.

"I guess not," her mom said with a chuckle and continued to season the chicken resting in a bowl. They were having fried chicken, candied yams, wild rice, mixed greens, green beans and cornbread.

She washed her hands and went to work slicing yams.

"How're you doing with the case?" her mother asked over her shoulder.

"Okay, I guess. We're supposed to be getting the rail in for inspection this week."

"Your father told me about how you put that lawyer in his place. He thinks you're going to be fantastic when it's time for you to take over the legal department."

Morgan groaned inwardly but didn't comment.

Her mother came over to the island where Morgan worked. "What's going on, sweetheart?"

"I just don't know if I want to spend my career working at the company. There are a lot of other opportunities I might want to explore."

"Nothing wrong with that. Any particular areas of practice you're thinking about?"

She'd been hoping to put this conversation off as long as possible. "Sports management."

"Really? I know you mentioned it growing up and when Malcolm started playing, but I didn't realize you were serious. Seems very few women are able to break into that field, especially pro football. Am I correct in assuming that's where your interest lies?"

"Yes."

"Well—"

"We're back!"

Morgan and her mother spun around, and her mother rushed over and engulfed Siobhan and Justin in a crushing hug.

"Hi, Mom," Siobhan said.

"Oh my goodness. I thought you weren't coming back until tonight."

Justin smiled and his teeth shone brightly in his clean-shaven mahogany face. "We got back last night and wanted to surprise you. Hey, Morgan."

"Hey. You guys look great." She hugged them. At five eight, Siobhan was an inch taller than Morgan and wore her hair in a short, curly style. Two weeks in Barbados had darkened her honey brown skin to a warm sienna color.

Her mother shooed Justin out. "Justin, Malcolm and Nolan are around here somewhere."

He chuckled. "I'm going." He placed a tender kiss on Siobhan's lips and left.

Morgan didn't miss the unspoken communication that passed between the two lovers. It immediately brought to mind the intense way Omar had been viewing her on Saturday at the fund-raiser and the conversation that followed. She'd had dreams about him savoring her like a dessert that left her throbbing and wanting.

"Morgan?" Siobhan playfully elbowed her. "You all right?"

"Fine. How was the honeymoon?" Siobhan and her mother gave Morgan a strange look. "What?"

"Mom just asked me that, and I said we had a great time. Where did your mind go?"

"Oh. I had a thought about work, that's all," she lied.

Siobhan frowned. "I hope you're not going to start doing like I did." Before she met Justin, Siobhan had been going overboard with her work hours in an attempt to prove she wasn't a disappointment to her parents. The unrealistic perception stemmed from a childhood incident Siobhan had blamed herself for, and its effects had carried over into adulthood. She was slowly learning to let go.

"I'm not. You're supposed to be telling us about all the fun you had," Morgan said, smoothly changing the subject, eager to have the spotlight off her.

Brandon and Khalil arrived just as dinner was being served. After her father recited the blessing, lively conversation commenced. Much of the talk centered on Siobhan and Justin's honeymoon. Later everyone sat around enjoying slices of homemade pound cake and laughing.

"Saw your picture in the paper today, Morgan," Brandon said casually.

Morgan froze.

"Oh?" her father asked.

Focusing on her cake, she said, "Probably from the fund-raiser I went to last night." She met Malcolm's gaze and offered a silent plea. He smiled and went back to his food.

"What kind of fund-raiser? Is it something we would be interested in making a donation to?"

"Actually, Dad, I was going to mention it to you next week. It's for a veterans' mental health center that's scheduled to open next March."

Brandon snorted. "I don't think that's the reason you were on the arm of Omar Drummond."

She shrugged. "He asked me to go. It was for a good cause."

"And the part about being his new agent?" Brandon asked, not looking up from his dessert.

"What?" The room exploded with questions, and Morgan wanted to disappear beneath the floor. As always, she looked to her twin for help.

Malcolm's sharp whistle cut through the noise. "Okay, everybody. Relax."

"Is it true, Morgan?" her mother asked.

"Yes."

Her father shook his head. "What about the case you're supposed to be handling?"

"This isn't going to affect me handling the case, Dad."

"We need all your focus on this case, Morgan," Brandon said. "I'm sure Drummond can find another agent if he needs one."

She whipped her head around and stared at him as if he had lost his mind. "No." An argument ensued, and after about two minutes she was done. She got up, took her plate to the kitchen and came back. "Can you take me home, Mal?"

Brandon stood and blocked her path. "We need to finish this."

Khalil, who had been silently observing, let out an exasperated sigh. "Sit down, Brandon. She said she could handle both." To Morgan he said, "I'm glad you're getting a chance to follow your dream, sis."

"Thanks."

"I'll call you later," Siobhan said.

Morgan nodded. She kissed her parents and strode out of the house. She rode silently behind Malcolm and hopped off the motorcycle as soon as he pulled up in front of her unit. "I'll see you later."

"You want to talk?"

"No. Maybe later."

He gave her a strong hug. "Don't worry about Brandon. You know how passionate he is when it comes to the company."

She nodded and headed for her door.

"I'll check on you later," Malcolm called out.

Morgan threw up a wave, went inside and placed her helmet on the coffee table. She was so mad she wanted to scream. Brandon had always been the most intense of the five siblings when it came to the company, and often acted like he already in charge. If he thought something or someone might interfere with its success, he tended to go overboard. He'd done the same thing with Siobhan when she first started dating Justin. But Morgan had no plans to follow through with Brandon's suggestion to have Omar find another agent. She was smart and driven. She multitasked well. She'd make it work to everyone's satisfaction, especially her parents'.

Her parents. Morgan dropped down on the sofa and released a deep sigh. She could see the questioning looks on their faces and knew she would have to call them later to explain. But not tonight. Tonight she just wanted to be left alone. Rising, she went to make some tea and settled at the kitchen table to work on Omar's contract.

An hour later, she heard the sound of a motorcycle and rolled her eyes. When Malcolm said he would check on her, she'd thought he meant he would call, not drive over. The doorbell rang as she stood. She hoped, it wouldn't take long to convince him she was okay. If he'd had a girlfriend, he would have had less time to be worried about Morgan.

Morgan snatched open the door, and her words died on her lips when she saw Omar standing there. With his hair held back by a band and wearing all black, he looked every bit of tall, dark and dangerously sexy. And although she shouldn't have been, she was happy to see him.

"Hey. Can I come in?"

She stepped back so he could enter and closed the door. "How did you get in? And what are you doing here?"

"Somebody was leaving the complex, so I drove in before the gate closed. And I came to see if you were okay."

"I'm fine. Why wouldn't I be?" She gestured him to a seat. He sat on the chair and she purposely chose the sofa.

"The photos in today's paper." He paused. "And I talked to Malcolm." He held up a hand when she opened her mouth. "Before you start in on your brother, he didn't call me. I called him because I was concerned, and he told me about what happened at your parent's house." Omar sat next to her and reached for her hand. "Morgan, I know your family is depending on you with the lawsuit, and I don't want your helping me out to cause problems with your job or your family."

"It's not, Omar. Trust me." Morgan eased her hand from his, leaned forward and braced her elbows on her knees. "I told my family a long time ago what I wanted to do. Except for Malcolm and my sister, Siobhan, everybody else figured it was something I'd said because I love football so much, especially after I went to law school and started working at the company. I'm not worried about my parents. They'll come around." She angled her head in his direction. "I appreciate the concern, but there's no need. Unless…you don't think I can do it." It dawned on her that, after talking to her brother, Omar might have some misgivings, just like her family. She met his eyes.

"It never crossed my mind that you wouldn't be able to accomplish both tasks. Not for one minute."

"Thank you." Their eyes held, and she saw the moment his gaze went from care and concern to something else. She wanted to look away but couldn't. She could feel the desire rising between them.

Finally he murmured, "It's not working, baby."

Morgan never even tried to pretend she didn't understand what he meant. He was right. And it hadn't been working since that first kiss in Malcolm's kitchen.

"Morgan, I…" Omar bent his head and let his kiss finish what he wanted to communicate.

She should have protested, should have pushed him away, but when his silky tongue slid between her lips to tangle with hers, protesting was the furthest thing from her mind. The kiss they'd shared before had lasted only a second or two, but this unhurried exploration of lips and tongues set her body aflame. His tongue made sweeping, swirling motions inside her mouth, then captured hers and sucked gently. Morgan moaned, shifted and straddled his thighs. She fisted her hands in his locs and took over the kiss, eliciting a low groan from him. Omar's big hands roamed down her back and caressed her buttocks. The bulge of his erection pressed firmly against her center. She broke off the kiss and realized how dangerously close she was to having sex with her client.

Omar rested his forehead against hers, his ragged breathing matching her own. "Please don't say this was a mistake."

Nothing about the kiss felt like a mistake. It felt like the most *right* thing she had done in a long time. "I won't."

He lifted his head and searched her face. A faint smile played around the corners of his mouth. "Nothing that happens between us will be a mistake."

"Omar—"

He silenced her with another kiss. "Nothing, baby."

"I'm not saying that. But I can't just go all out and start dating you."

"Why not?"

She leaned back and gave him a sidelong glance. "You're kidding, right? You just told people *last night* that I was your agent. What do you think they're going to say when they find out we're seeing each other? Let me help you with the answer. They're going to say I'm sleeping my way into the business." Morgan left his lap and reclaimed her spot on the sofa.

"Then what do you suggest we do? Because me not kissing you again isn't an option."

She had never experienced such pleasure from a kiss, so in reality, it wasn't an option for her, either. "We keep it a secret for as long as possible, preferably until after your contract negotiation is done."

"Roughly six weeks."

She nodded.

Omar shrugged. "Sounds good in theory."

"But…"

"But, you know what happens whenever you walk anywhere within my line of sight. You said it yourself…my favorite dessert."

Morgan picked up one of the pillows next to her and swatted him with it. "You're not helping, Drummond."

"Maybe not, but I'm being honest."

"Yeah, well, all this honesty is going to put you back where you were two days ago…with *no* kisses."

"I definitely don't want that to happen," he said with a laugh and mimicked zipping his lips.

She rolled her eyes. "Whatever."

Still chuckling, he pulled her into his arms. "In all seriousness, I get what you're saying and I respect it, so when we're out, I'll do my best to keep it professional."

"Thank you."

"But…since we're not in public right now…"

When he covered her mouth and gave her another long, intoxicating kiss, Morgan couldn't have been happier that they were not in public.

Omar fed on Morgan's luscious kisses and marveled at how well her mouth fit with his. As he'd told her, he liked to savor his desserts, and he took his time sampling her sweetness. He sucked and licked every delicious inch of her mouth. Her taste was addictive and he couldn't get enough. The sound of her low moans in his ear and the way she returned his kiss with equal fervor fueled his passions, and he grew harder with each sensual moment. Reaching up, he removed the band holding her hair in a ponytail. The curly dark brown and golden-highlighted strands fell like a curtain around her face, and he sucked in a sharp breath. He was on the brink of losing control and forced himself to rein in his runaway desire. "We should probably slow down. Otherwise we're going to end up in your bed," he murmured, still trailing kisses along her jaw.

"Mmm, you're probably right," Morgan said.

Omar stared into her honey-brown eyes and couldn't resist one more. He leaned back against the sofa, tightened his arm around her and closed his eyes, willing his body to a calmer state.

"You probably think I'm a bad hostess. I didn't even offer you anything to drink."

"You're not a bad hostess at all. And you offered me something much sweeter."

She moved out of his embrace and stood. "This line of conversation is going to put us right back in dangerous territory."

He came to his feet, slid an arm around her waist and nuzzled her neck. "Yep, but I can't seem to help myself when I'm around you."

She laughed. "Mmm-hmm, knock it off. You've gotten all the kisses you're getting for tonight. Now, do you want something to drink?" Morgan took his hand and led him to her kitchen.

He noticed papers spread on the kitchen table and a half-filled mug. "I didn't realize you'd been working. Sorry."

"It's no biggie. I was just checking stats, doing some calculations and making notations."

Omar peered into the cup, but because of the mug's dark coloring he couldn't determine the contents. "Are you drinking coffee this late in the day?"

"No, mint tea. I'm not a big coffee drinker. The only coffee addict in our family is Brandon. What about you?"

"I drink it sometimes, but I try to keep my intake down, especially when I'm training. Then it's mostly water."

"I have some iced tea."

"Can I get a rain check? I should get going. I had only planned to stop by for a minute to check on you."

"Sure."

"Walk me out?"

At the door, she gestured toward his motorcycle. "Nice bike."

"I'll take you riding anytime you want."

"I'd like that."

Omar knew he should leave, but he couldn't get his feet to move.

"You're looking at me like that again," Morgan said with amusement.

"I'm going." He placed a quick kiss on her lips. "See you later. Lock up."

"I will."

Letting his gaze roam over her face once more, he turned and loped down the walkway. He wanted nothing more than to make love to her, but the last time he jumped into a relationship with both feet, he had come away with both his reputation and his heart in shreds. He needed to slow down. It would be a huge undertaking, but this time he planned to proceed with caution.

Chapter 8

Monday evening, Morgan made it to the dance studio fifteen minutes before her class began. She rushed into the dressing room and changed out of her navy suit and into her dancewear. She waved to Brooke, whose tap class was in the middle of practicing Michael Jackson's "Jam," and continued to her classroom.

"Hey, guys," she called out to the students.

"Hi, Ms. Gray," they chorused.

One student said, "I didn't know that our Michael Jackson song is from 1979. That's *old*."

Morgan laughed. She guessed that to a thirteen-year-old, any song older than five years would be considered old. She and Brooke wanted to highlight the many facets the popular performer's music and had included songs that spanned his forty-plus-year career, choosing "Burn This Disco Out" from his *Off the Wall* album for Morgan's hip-hop dance class. "Okay, everybody. Let me see what you've got."

The students got into their positions, and Morgan started the music. She walked the room, correcting where needed and giving the thumbs up when they mastered a section of the song. By the end of the class, the students performed the piece without one misstep.

After dismissing the class, Brooke sauntered over. "I like it."

"So do I."

"I hope the dances you and I do turn out as well."

"Girl, that's no problem for you. Me, on the other

hand…" Morgan shook her head. "I'm still a little leery about getting on the stage."

"You'll do fine. Let's see it. What song did you choose?"

Fiddling with her iPod, she mumbled, "'I Can't Help It.'"

"Hmm. Okay." Brooke came over and eased it from Morgan's hand. "You get into position and I'll start it."

She nodded, moved to the center of the room and positioned herself. The music started and she went through the choreographed moves. At the end, she turned to Brooke. "Well?"

"The moves are all there, but you're missing the passion. Stop holding back, Morgan. Feel the music."

"Okay." She closed her eyes and took a deep breath. "Start it again." This time, she let the music take over and focused on the lyrics. Soon she was lost, and thoughts of the kisses she and Omar shared last night emerged. The chorus summed up the emotional struggle she had been battling. She told him she'd see him in private, but after he'd left, she wondered if it was the right decision. But she didn't know if she would be able to fight her growing attraction toward him any longer. Or if she really wanted to anymore.

"Now *that's* what I'm talking about," Brooke said with a huge grin when the song ended. "I could feel the emotional pull. I knew you hadn't lost your edge." She threw her arms around Morgan. "If the kids' performances don't pull in some money, yours definitely will."

Morgan laughed. "You're laying it on pretty thick, aren't you? I already said I'd do the dance." While the studio had a good number of paying students, Brooke wanted to be able to offer classes to all students and didn't want money to be a barrier. The money raised would go a long way in helping to expand classes and provide funds to hire two more teachers. Brooke also had plans to purchase the newly vacated building next door to create a larger studio.

"Yeah, but I know you. You said the same thing last year but changed your mind."

"You would bring that up."

Brooke gave her a sidelong glance.

"I promise I won't change my mind."

"Good. Now tell me what's going on with you and Mr. Sexy."

"There's nothing going on," she said.

"No? That dance tells me things are heating up. And please don't try to tell me it's nothing." Brooke laughed. "This is the point where I say 'I told you so' about that no-kissing rule."

Heat stung her cheeks. "Everything was going according to plan until last night. He's working to open a mental health center for veterans and plans to be on staff as a clinical psychologist when his football career is over. I went with him to a fund-raiser for the center this past weekend."

"You went as his date?" Brooke asked with surprise. She pulled out her phone and started typing.

"No, as his agent. It was sort of our announcement. Anyway, some pictures showed up in the paper yesterday, and Brandon saw them." She gave Brooke the details of the blowup at the family dinner. "I could've killed him. I wanted to tell them in my own time, but now it's a mess. My parents didn't look too happy about it, especially my dad. I know he's thinking my taking on Omar will interfere with me handling the lawsuit."

"I'm sure your parents will come around. And these photos were nice. You two look good together." She held up her phone briefly, then went back to reading. "The article seemed to question Omar's sanity for dumping someone who's considered to be the agent of agents."

"Yeah, and it didn't help that said agent showed up and tried to make a scene."

Brooke's eyes went wide. *"Really?"*

Morgan nodded and rubbed a hand across her forehead. "Called me out of my name, threatened Omar."

"I'm surprised I didn't read about the man being punched in the face. It has happened before," Brooke added.

She smiled. "Believe me, I wanted to. I had a hard time restraining myself." In high school, one of the more popular football players had tried coming on to Morgan. She'd turned him down flat because he had a reputation for sleeping around and getting rough with some of the girls. He made the mistake of getting in her face and calling her a name, and Morgan sent him home with a black eye. She had worked hard over the years to learn to keep her temper in check. "Instead, I told him he'd be in court if he said anything about me or my client."

"See, I miss all the good stuff."

"It was fine up to that point. I got a couple of sideways looks, but other than that…" She shrugged.

Brooke waved a hand. "Back to the good stuff. Sounds like Mr. Drummond might have some potential."

"Maybe. I thought he was like most of the other playboy athletes, but the more I learn about him and spend time with him, the more I'm starting to like him. You should've heard him speak. He was *amazing*. It was a totally different side of him that the media has never shown."

"So, what are you going to do?"

Morgan sighed. "I agreed to see him in private until after his new contract is signed, but I'm starting to wonder if it might be a bad idea."

"You just said he's not at all what you expected based on the media, so I don't understand why it's a bad idea."

"He's still an athlete," she said with a pointed look. Her pro basketball player boyfriend had turned out to be arrogant enough for ten people. He'd foolishly believed that Morgan would stand by while he entertained groupies when on the road, and had the audacity to tell her, "Hey, it's not like I'm going to see them again. It's you I'm coming home to." She promised herself she would never date another athlete, but was now on the cusp of breaking her own vow. She gathered up her belongings and followed Brooke out.

Brooke stopped at the space she used as an office. "Not all athletes are the same, Morgan."

"I know. But, remember—" Her cell buzzed in her hand, preempting what she planned to say. Morgan looked down at the display and saw Omar's number. "Speaking of." She connected the call. "Hey, Omar."

"Hey, beautiful. Is this a bad time?"

"No. What's up?"

"I have a proposition for you. You said we could be together in private, correct?"

"Yes," she said warily.

"Come away with me this weekend to my cabin."

"Your cabin in the mountains?" she blurted before remembering Brooke was still standing there. Brooke folded her arms, and a sly smile spread across her lips. Morgan shot her a look. "Um… I don't know, Omar."

"We can discuss the contract. You asked me if I was going to be around next weekend so we could talk, didn't you?"

"Yes, but—"

"Then it's perfect. We can talk without being interrupted, and you can get things done on your case from work if you want, too."

"Can I let you know in a couple of days?" She really needed to think about being alone with him in the mountains. Just the thought made her heart beat faster.

"All right. Will it help if I promise to let you set the pace? No denying I want to make love to you, but only when you're ready."

Her eyes slid closed. "Yeah, it helps."

"I *am* going to need at least two kisses a day, though," Omar said with a chuckle.

Morgan smiled. "I have to go. I'll call you."

"Night, baby."

"Good night." She ended the call and glanced over at Brooke's smiling face. "Don't say one word, Brooke Alexander."

"I wasn't going to say anything," she said with feigned innocence.

"I'm going home."

"See you on Thursday for the dress rehearsal."

"Okay. I like the idea of doing it a week earlier instead of the day before. Gives us a couple more rehearsals to iron out all the kinks."

"Me, too. That's why I chose to change it for this year. Last year, the kids were frantic about not having enough time to fix mistakes. It also means you'll have time to work out the kinks in yours. And after that phone call, I can't see you having any problems with a flawless performance. You should invite Omar to the show."

"No way. He doesn't even know about this place."

"I, for one, think he'd *really* enjoy that dance. You've already kissed him and agreed to see him, so…"

"I thought you weren't going to say anything." Animated voices rounded the corner and called out greetings, which she and Brooke returned.

"I didn't say anything. Gotta go." Brooke strolled off with a wave.

Muttering under her breath about traitorous best friends, Morgan pushed through the door and was met with a warm breeze. Despite it being eight in the evening, the July heat had not totally abated.

As she drove home, Omar's offer weighed heavily on her mind. She appreciated him allowing her to set the limits, but they both knew if she decided to go, it would signal a change in their relationship.

"Hey, Mom," Omar said into the cell as he got out of his car and walked across the lot to the Cobras' practice facility. Inside, he nodded at the front desk staff, went through a door leading down a hallway and mouthed greetings to his teammates. He exited out the back and took the tunnel leading to the practice field.

"Hello, Omar. I was calling to see if you were still alive since I haven't heard from you."

"It's only been a couple of weeks."

"Well, that's two weeks too long."

He chuckled. "I'll try to get by the restaurant or the house soon. I promise."

"All right."

"Love you."

"I love you, too. Don't make me have to put out a search and rescue call."

"I won't," he said laughing and said his goodbyes. When Rashad went into the service and wasn't able to communicate with the family consistently, she worried constantly. So when Omar left for college, she insisted on him checking in at least every couple of weeks. Years later, she still expected him and his brother to check in.

Omar went out and stood on the sidelines to watch the practice. While he and the other veterans didn't have to report to camp for another two weeks, he liked to get a sense of the new players' strengths and weaknesses. He saw Marcus jogging in his direction.

"I see you're doing the same thing I am," Marcus said when he reached Omar.

"Yeah. How's it going?"

"I don't know. Still a little worried about the other receiver position. Colin's not going to be ready."

"Really?"

"Yeah, I just talked to him." They watched a second-string receiver miss an easy pass and groaned. "You may be filling in this season, too," Marcus cracked.

Omar chuckled. "We'll see."

"Were you able to get in touch with my brother?"

He nodded. "Thanks. I hadn't thought about contacting him initially because I assumed he was an agent."

"Jae? He doesn't have the patience. I barely convinced him to do my contract. Speaking of agents, I heard you have a new one."

"You heard right."

"I don't know how Morgan is as an agent, but the woman has a hell of a game. I couldn't believe she intercepted that pass at Malcolm's picnic. I didn't even see her until she'd snatched the ball out of the air." He shook his head. "Instead of her being your agent, maybe we ought to see about signing her."

He laughed. "She'd love that." He had never met a woman who enjoyed football as much as he did.

Marcus shook his head and sighed again. Gesturing toward the field, he said, "I think this young fella needs some help. I'll catch you later. Oh, let me know how it works out with Morgan. If she's half as good an agent as she is a player, I might have to fire my brother."

Grinning, Omar said, "I'll keep you posted." While most people had been cordial when he'd introduced Morgan as his new agent, Marcus was the first person who didn't question the change or consider her a liability.

"Hey, Drummond."

He shifted his attention to the man who had joined him. "What's up, Colin? How's the knee?"

Colin blew out a long breath. "For some reason there's still some swelling, and my range of motion is at minus eighteen degrees. The doc won't sign off and says I'll miss preseason and probably the first few games of the regular season."

"That's a tough break. Sorry to hear it." With Colin coming up on age thirty-five, Omar realized it might be harder for the receiver to make a comeback.

"Yeah, me, too. I was counting on at least being back by the end of preseason." They watched a couple of plays. Then Colin asked, "What's this I hear about you and a new agent? Do you think it was wise to switch so close to contract time, especially with a shark like Roland? You were a big part of the reason we made it to the conference championship last season, and management knows it. I don't know if I'd trust my future to someone with no experience, especially a woman. I mean, what does she really know about football?"

Omar clenched his teeth. "Then it's a good thing you aren't me. I trust her and that's all that matters. And as far as the game, she knows it as well as you and I do. Good luck with the knee." He sauntered over to the other side of the field to place as much distance between him and his teammate as possible before he was tempted to say something he shouldn't. He was tired of people telling him he'd made a mistake by choosing Morgan as his agent. So far, he had managed to keep his cool, but if one more person made a disparaging comment about her, all bets were off.

Chapter 9

Two days later, Morgan still hadn't decided whether to accompany Omar to his mountain retreat. Getting away for a couple of days was tempting, especially considering the week she'd had. She still hadn't spoken to Brandon and walked on eggshells around her father. She arrived in the conference room twenty minutes ahead of the nine o'clock meeting time with Mr. Porter and sat sipping her tea.

"Hey."

She looked up fleetingly at Brandon standing in the doorway and went back to her tea. "Hey."

Brandon took a seat next to her at the table. He braced his arms on the polished mahogany wood and stared out the large window that covered one wall for several seconds before speaking. "How long are you going to give me the silent treatment?"

"Who says I'm giving you the silent treatment? I've been busy."

"That's a bunch of bull and you know it."

"Is it? Are you sure it wasn't you giving me the silent treatment?"

His jaw tightened. "Look, I'm sorry." He scrubbed a hand over his face. "First Vonnie, now you," he muttered. "I seem to be batting zero with you two when it comes to this case." When the suit was initially filed, Siobhan had gone to Las Vegas with Justin and didn't receive Brandon's urgent phone calls until the next day. He'd been upset and insinuated that she should have been available. "Maybe I was a little over the top, but you should have told us first."

Morgan raised an eyebrow. "A little? And that's exactly

why I hadn't said anything. Besides, it just happened a couple of weeks ago."

"But Malcolm knew?"

"Yes."

"Good morning, Brandon and Morgan."

She and Brandon greeted their quality assurance specialist, John Bledsoe. He introduced Mr. Metzler, the representative from the third-party company who would be testing the faulty rail alongside them.

"We'll continue this conversation later," Brandon whispered to her.

Morgan eyed him and whispered back, "There's nothing to continue. It's a done deal." She rose and went to call the receptionist to see whether Mr. Porter had arrived. The attorney showed up at half past nine and strolled in as if he had all the time in the world.

"For a moment, we thought you weren't coming, Mr. Porter," Morgan said. "You seem to be missing something."

"You know how this LA traffic can be. Missing?"

It is too early in the morning to deal with this kind of foolishness. "The rail."

"Oh, it's in my car. There was no way to manage carrying it and—"

"Let's go," Brandon said, cutting him off and impatiently rising to his feet.

The attorney opened his mouth to say something, but with Brandon towering over him by a good six inches and glaring, he thought better of it and mumbled something that sounded like, "Be right back."

They returned ten minutes later and carefully laid everything on the table. Morgan took pictures of the rail at different angles, as well as the packaging—inside and out. The attorney had given the impression that the rail had broken apart, and she was slightly surprised to find that it hadn't. Her suspicions rose even higher, and she made sure to capture every inch on film.

John did a visual inspection of the rail. "At first glance, it looks intact and I can't see why it would've come away from the wall, especially if it had been installed properly."

"Are you accusing my clients of something?" Mr. Porter asked.

"Not at all, sir. I won't know anything until the tests are complete."

Apparently the answer didn't satisfy the attorney because he ignored John and said, "Mr. Metzler, I trust you'll be conducting your own tests. I want to ensure there will be some neutrality."

"Yes."

Morgan did a mental eye roll and said tightly, "Mr. Porter, that's why Mr. Metzler is here." She faced John. "How long do you think the tests will take?"

"No more than a day or two, and I can have the report in a week."

She nodded and turned her attention to the other man. "Mr. Metzler?"

"Reports are typically completed in two to three weeks."

"And if we request expedited service?"

"A week to ten days."

"That works. Mr. Porter, we'll call and schedule a time to meet once the results are in. Do you have any other questions or concerns before we adjourn?"

"No. I'm looking forward to getting this settled."

"As are we." Morgan stood and extended her hand. "Thank you for coming. We'll be in touch."

Brandon followed suit. "I appreciate your coming." Once the conference room cleared out, he propped a hip on the table and folded his arms. "What do think about that rail?"

"Frankly, I was surprised. Porter made it sound like

the rail had snapped in half. I didn't see one crack in it, so there has to be another reason why it failed. I'm wondering even more what he's up to."

"I didn't notice anything, either. I have this gnawing feeling that Porter's trying to pull one over on us, and I don't like it."

"If he is, we'll know when the tests are complete. I'll probably call John on Friday to see if he can give me some preliminary results. "

"Let me know once you get them."

"I will."

"Can I ask you something?"

Morgan had a feeling this had nothing to do with work. "What?"

"How serious are you about this whole agent thing?"

"I've been talking about this for years, Brandon."

"I guess I always thought it was a passing phase."

"It's not. I really want to do this."

He nodded. "I'm more curious about how you managed to land one of the best players in the league. Most people start out with second- and third-string players, but not my baby sister."

Morgan chuckled. "Hey, you know what they say—go big or go home. Actually, he came to me." She saw Brandon's questioning look and added, "And I'm not at liberty to discuss any particulars about his former agent." She figured the details would headline the sports news soon enough.

Brandon studied her for a moment. "Okay. But if Roland Foster gets in your face again—"

"You'll do nothing," she said, cutting him off. "Should I expect a call from Khalil, too? You can save him the trouble and pass along the same message. You guys taught Siobhan and me how to stand up and fight for ourselves, so when are you going to let us do it?"

"Probably never," he said with a wry chuckle.

She shook her head. "I can handle this. But if I get into trouble, I promise to let you know. Deal?"

"Yeah, deal." He straightened from the table, hugged her and placed a kiss on her temple. "I suppose you're not that same little twelve-year-old girl running behind Malcolm with your stat sheets anymore."

"I still have my stat sheets, only this time I'll be putting them to good use." They quieted for a moment. "Well, I want to get these photos printed and start going through them." She picked up the camera. "See you later."

"Morgan."

Brandon's voice stopped her as she reached the door. She turned back.

"No matter what, I'm proud of you, sis."

She smiled. "Thanks." Her smile was still in place when she made it back to her office. Even the frown on Evelyn's face couldn't ruin her mood.

As soon as Morgan sat down, Siobhan knocked and poked her head in the door.

"Can I come in?"

"Of course." Morgan stood and the two sisters embraced. "You look so relaxed and happy."

Siobhan smiled. "I am. Didn't think I'd ever be, but I'm glad Justin came into my life." Siobhan had been previously engaged until she found out that her fiancé had stolen money from her bank account, and she overheard him talking marriage to another woman three weeks before their wedding. "Anyway, I didn't come to talk about me. I see a lot happened while I was gone. How are you doing?"

The older she got, the more Morgan appreciated her sister. She'd always been supportive and often helped Morgan think things through. "I'm okay."

"You were pretty mad on Sunday. That's why I wanted to give you a few days before my inquisition." They shared a smile. "How did you land Omar Drummond as a client? Most people don't get the A-listers out of the gate."

"Unless that A-lister comes to you."

Siobhan's eyebrows shot up. *"Really?"*

She nodded. "I can't give you too many specifics, although I'm sure you'll be reading about them soon, but he was having problems and wanted someone new."

"And he came to you. As great a player as he is, he could've easily found a far more experienced agent. So, again, why you—someone who has never negotiated a contract and is a woman, to boot?"

"This wasn't the first time he's had bad luck with an agent." Morgan filled Siobhan in on what Omar had shared about his first agent's terrible contract negotiation and the few details she knew about the scandal surrounding his ex after the second agent left Omar hanging. "He said he wanted someone who had no ties to the league."

"That's understandable. I think I'd feel the same way. And I know you won't have any problems negotiating him a great contract."

"I hope so. Thanks, Vonnie. That means a lot coming from you."

Siobhan smiled. "So, how are you two dealing with that sizzling attraction between you? Dating a client—your *first* client, that is—might look a little suspicious."

Blunt as always. Siobhan had never been one to bite her tongue and could reduce a grown man to tears. "Who says we're attracted to each other?" Morgan asked casually while plugging the USB cable into the computer.

Siobhan gave Morgan a pointed look, crossed her arms and waited.

"I told him we could only see each other secretly until his contract is finalized," she muttered reluctantly.

"And he agreed?"

Morgan nodded.

"But you're having a hard time with that decision, huh?" Siobhan said with a chuckle.

She gave a careless shrug. "What makes you think it's a problem?"

"Look at the man. You can't tell me you don't want to rip his clothes off and run your hands all over that hard-as-a-rock body every time you see him." She leaned forward and added, "Girl, I remember that commercial. *Yummy!*" She sat back and fanned herself.

Morgan's face heated, and she fumbled with the papers on the desk.

"I'll ask again. Having problems?"

Morgan tried to maintain the facade but failed. "Oh my goodness, *yes*," she said with a groan.

Siobhan laughed. "That's what I thought."

"He invited me to spend this weekend with him at his cabin," she blurted without thought, and immediately wanted to snatch the words back.

"I understand you guys know each other from Malcolm's get-togethers, but this seems to be moving fast. Did I miss something else?"

She also felt like things were moving fast but had no control over the situation. "He kissed me when we were at Malcolm's barbecue." She shared what led up to the kiss. "Omar mentioned wanting to talk to me, but after he kissed me, I avoided him for the rest of the afternoon. It wasn't until he showed up here the next day that he asked me to be his agent."

Siobhan stood. "I need to get back to my office, but if you do decide to go, have fun…and be careful. It was one of those out-of-town trips that made me realize I was falling for Justin. See you later." She walked to the door and turned back. "Oh, and knock the Cobras management team's socks off."

Morgan chuckled and waved. Although she wasn't necessarily seeking their approval, it was nice to know Brandon and Siobhan had her back. Their conversations played over in her mind as she uploaded the pictures. She had known they would be curious about how she acquired Omar as a client. Morgan still couldn't believe her good fortune. With all the available sports agents out there, he'd come to her.

Her gaze strayed to the flash drive on her desk. She had spotted it this morning near the edge of the coffee table and didn't recognize it. She plugged it into her laptop and realized it belonged to Omar when she saw the various files relating to the mental health center. It must have fallen out of his pocket when he was at her place on Sunday. She pulled out her cell and sent him a quick text to let him know she'd found it.

Morgan was in the middle of printing out the pictures of the rail when her cell buzzed. She read Omar's reply:

I've been looking all over for it. I can come by tonight to pick it up after you get off.

She and Brooke were going to dinner and spending the evening deciding the order of the dance production numbers, and she didn't know how late it would be when they finished. She typed back:

Having dinner and late meeting tonight. Can I drop it off tomorrow after work around 5?

That works. Thanks.

If she left work early as planned tomorrow, she could drop off the flash drive and be at the studio no later than five-forty-five to get ready for the dress rehearsal performance scheduled to start at seven. The visit would serve a two-fold mission because she had decided to spend the weekend with him.

The next evening, Omar pulled Morgan into his house, shut the door and crushed his mouth against hers. He'd been waiting to kiss her since he left her house on Sunday. She met him stroke for stroke. Her soft curves against him sent heat thrumming through his body. He pressed her against the door and continued to devour her mouth while his hands slid down her torso and over her hips. He banded his arms around her waist and brought her even closer.

"Omar," Morgan whispered against his lips.

Hearing her call him by his first name always did something to him. He gifted her with one last kiss then set her on her feet. "Hi."

"Hi." She handed him the flash drive. "I can't stay."

He pocketed it and tried to hide his disappointment, but the smile on her face said he hadn't been successful.

She reached up and massaged his face. "If your jaw gets any tighter, it's going to shatter. Stop pouting. Would it make you feel better if I told you I decided to go with you this weekend to your cabin?"

A smile bloomed on his face. "Yeah. Would it be too hard for you to leave work a little early? I want to stop at the store and get up there before dark. I'd like to be on the road around three. There will probably be traffic anyway, but if we leave too much later, it'll be worse."

"It shouldn't be a problem since I'm bringing some work with me." Morgan glanced down at her watch. "I need to get going. I promised Brooke I'd be there to help her before six."

"I'll walk you out."

When they got to the driveway, she threw up her hands and muttered an unladylike curse.

Omar frowned. "What's wrong?"

"My tire. I don't have time for this." She remembered hitting something on the road but hadn't thought anything of it.

"I can change it."

Morgan paced in front of him. "I need to leave now if I'm going to make it on time."

He placed his hands on her shoulders. "Relax. I can take you where you need to go. I just need to grab my keys and wallet." A brief look of panic crossed her face, giving him pause. Was she going to meet some other man? They hadn't mentioned having an exclusive relationship, but he assumed it was a given after the first kiss.

After a few seconds, she nodded. "Okay."

Not knowing where they were headed, Omar took a quick minute to change from his shorts and tank top to a pair of jeans and pullover tee. He exited through the garage and backed out his truck. Morgan tossed a duffel bag in the back and climbed in, still frowning.

"Are we leaving?" she asked when he didn't start driving.

"Ah, as soon as you tell me where I'm going," he said with a smile.

She finally smiled, too. "That would help, huh?" She gave him an address in Culver City. "Take the 405 to the 10. That way we can cut out a little bit of the traffic."

From his Brentwood home, the drive would normally take about fifteen minutes without traffic. But at this time of day—no matter what day of the week it was—the commute would most likely be doubled. As he drove, he stole glances at Morgan. She hadn't said one word in the twenty minutes they'd been on the road aside from giving him the address. She sat with her arms folded, staring out the window, but not even her tightly set features could distract from her beauty. As pretty as he found her, he was even more turned on by her brain and fortitude. He smiled every time he thought about how she had handled the confrontation with Roland.

"Is there some reason you're being so secretive about where we're going? Do I need to be worried?"

Morgan turned his way. "No to both questions." She hesitated, then said, "We're going to a local theater. My friend Brooke runs a dance studio, and tonight is the dress rehearsal. The kids are going to be performing for their parents."

"What kind of classes does she offer?"

"Ballet, tap, jazz, hip-hop...a little of everything."

"Sounds interesting. My niece just mentioned wanting to take a dance class."

"What kind?"

"I have no idea. We didn't get that far in the conversation." Serena had confided in Omar that they couldn't afford the classes. Omar wanted to tell her that he would pay for it but held back out of respect for his brother. He planned to ask Rashad about it the next time they spoke.

The Essence Theater was only four blocks from the freeway. The brick building looked like a throwback from another era. "Is that your friend's studio?" He pointed to a modern building across the street from the theater.

"Yes. You can just drop me off in front. I'll have Brooke bring me back to your house to pick up my car after the show, if you're okay with her knowing where you live."

Omar ignored her and parked. He got out, came around to her side and helped her out.

Morgan quickly let go of his hand. "Thanks for the ride." She stared up at him.

"I'm trying hard to not to break our agreement, but the way you're looking at me is going to get you kissed."

She glanced up and down the street. "Well, if we make

it quick, nobody will see." She came up on tiptoe and brushed a kiss on his lips. "I gotta go. I'm already late."

Omar stood there smiling, his gaze following the sweet sway of her hips and the long strides of her shapely legs in the slim skirt as she rushed off. He walked around to the driver's side, opened the door and then closed it again. Curious, he went to check out the show.

Inside the small theater that looked to hold roughly two hundred people, he saw a couple dozen people seated in the front and Morgan on the stage talking to a slender woman. A few teenagers stood off to the side practicing a dance step. The women left the stage, and he sauntered down the aisle and took an end seat a few rows behind the group of people, grateful he'd had the foresight to change clothes. The audience continued to filter in until about one quarter of the theater was filled. Several minutes later, the lights went down, and the woman he had seen talking to Morgan came out to the center of the stage.

"Good evening and welcome to the show. For those who don't know me, I'm Brooke Alexander, owner of the Creative Flow Dance Studio, located right across the street. You are in for a real treat. Your children have worked hard and I am very proud of what they've accomplished, as I'm sure you will be."

Omar listened as she thanked the parents and talked about her vision for the coming year. He tuned back in when Morgan, another woman and a man joined Brooke onstage.

"I'd like to take a moment to thank these three special people," Brooke continued. "Without them, this program wouldn't be possible." She introduced the man and woman as teachers of the beginning hip-hop and ballet classes, respectively. She reached for Morgan's hand. "This lady here is my best friend, my right hand and the one who keeps me sane." The audience laughed and Morgan smiled. "She also teaches the jazz and advanced hip-hop classes."

Omar sat up straight. Morgan *taught* dance. She'd given him the impression that she only *helped.* Attorney, sports agent and now dance teacher… He didn't know what to expect next. He had originally planned to stay for one or two dance routines to see if this might be something Brianna would like. However, he had no intensions of leaving until the end. With a smile, Omar made himself comfortable and prepared to enjoy the show.

He found he more than enjoyed the show, especially the Michael Jackson theme. They danced to songs he hadn't heard since he was a kid and ones his parents used to play. He hummed along and rocked his head to the beat. His niece would definitely thrive in this environment, and he made a mental note to get information on classes from Morgan.

Brooke appeared onstage again and he started to stand, thinking the show had ended.

"Let's give the students another hand." She waited until the applause faded. "This year we've added a special segment I like to call Instructor Showcase. Dancing to 'I Can't Help It,' I present Morgan Gray."

Omar froze. The curtain opened, and there Morgan stood posed under a spotlight center stage. The music began and he slowly lowered himself back into the seat, transfixed by her sensual movements. The form-fitting tank top and pants revealed every curve in her toned body. His arousal was immediate. As she continued to execute high kicks, leaps and quick turns, he grew harder and shifted in his seat. By the time the last note faded, he was breathing as if he'd run an eighty-yard touchdown.

He closed his eyes, inhaled deeply and released the breath slowly. He prayed the lights stayed low until he could bring his body under control. The other instructors' performances were nice, but he could not get the vision of Morgan's sleek body out of his mind.

By the time the lights came up and all the students and instructors took their final bow, his body was somewhat calmer. Omar rose to his feet with the rest of the audience in a standing ovation. Because of his height, it didn't take long for Morgan's stunned gaze to connect with his. His mouth inched up in a smile. The evening was about to get very interesting.

Chapter 10

Morgan almost passed out when she saw Omar in the audience. What was he still doing here? She thought he'd gone home. *Oh, God! Did he see me dance?*

Brooke bumped her shoulder and whispered, "What is wrong with you?"

She whipped her head around and realized everyone was leaving the stage to greet their family members. "Nothing. I'm fine." She hazarded a glimpse in Omar's direction again and found him still smiling.

"You sure? You looked a little freaked out for a minute."

"Positive."

"Oo-kay," Brooke said, seemingly not convinced. "Let's get these tickets passed out so I can take you back to get your car before it gets too late."

"That won't be necessary," Morgan mumbled, watching as Omar sauntered toward the stage.

"I thought you… Oh my word. Is that *Omar Drummond* coming this way?"

Still staring in his direction, Morgan answered, "Yeah, that's him."

"Seeing him on the TV screen did *not* come close to doing him justice," Brooke said in awe. "That man is fine, fine, *fine!*"

Morgan turned back and waved her hand in front of Brooke's face. "I thought you wanted to give the parents their tickets."

"You're inviting him to the show and reception, right?"

"Ah, I hadn't planned to. I never actually told him I teach at the studio…or dance."

Brooke laughed. "Well, *that* cat is out of the bag. And by the look on his face, I'd say he really enjoyed your dance."

Morgan skewered her friend with a look.

Brooke just smiled. "I'll take care of the tickets. You go see about Mr. Drummond." She narrowed her gaze. "And you'd better not leave without introducing us or I am going to seriously hurt you."

Morgan shook her head and went to meet Omar.

"Hey. I thought you went home."

"I was going to stay for only a couple of dances, you know, for my niece, but I got caught up in the show. It was great. And you...you were *incredible*, amazing. Why didn't you tell me you were a dancer?"

Still in shock that he'd seen her performance, she ran a shaky hand over her ragged ponytail. "I don't know. I used to dance in school, but I'm not a dancer."

"I like the MJ theme and the song you danced to... I heard and felt everything you were trying to convey. It was as if you were dancing just for me, and I'm right with you, baby."

Her breath hitched. How had he known? From the first note to the last, he had been running through her mind. And like the lyrics said, she couldn't help it. "We're in public," Morgan reminded him.

Omar leaned down close to her ear. "And that's the only reason you aren't naked in my arms, my hand and mouth caressing every part of your body as I take us on a trip to heaven." He straightened and stepped back.

His hushed promise sent a rush of desire through her. The heat in his magnetic gaze seduced and tempted her to forget all about her request to keep their relationship a secret. "I... It shouldn't take too long for us to finish up."

"No rush. I'll sit here and wait for you."

Morgan nodded, unable to look away.

"Ms. Gray?"

She spun around at the sound of her name being called, and tried to focus on what the teen was saying. She gave the young woman instructions needed for next week's schedule, then helped Brooke and the other two instructors, Kay and Roy, make sure the theater was returned to its former state.

Brooke all but rushed Kay and Roy out the door, then dragged Morgan over to where Omar sat waiting.

Omar rose to his feet at their approach.

"Omar, this my friend Brooke Alexander. Brooke, Omar Drummond."

"It's a pleasure to meet you, Ms. Alexander."

"The pleasure is all mine, Mr. Drummond, and please call me Brooke."

"Only if you call me Omar. You have some talented students and instructors," he added, shifting his focus to Morgan.

A rush of heat stung Morgan's face.

Brook viewed them knowingly. "Thank you. We have a good group of kids. If you're not busy next Friday, I hope you can join us for the actual performance as well as the reception. It's a fund-raiser. Morgan can fill you in on the details."

Morgan wanted to pop her friend.

Omar nodded. "I wouldn't miss it."

"You'll need a ticket for both events." Brooke handed them to him, then said to Morgan, "Since you don't need a ride, I'm going to head out."

Morgan noted the amusement on Brooke's face. "We're leaving, too." She retrieved her duffel from the dressing room and followed Omar out to his truck.

"I can't get over that dance," Omar said as he drove them back to his place. "You're a really great dancer. I'm surprised you didn't pursue that as a career."

"Thanks, but dancing was just fun for me in school.

Brooke, on the other hand, was phenomenal, and a career in dance was a natural transition for her."

"Has she danced professionally or has she always been a dance teacher?"

"She danced for five years and was amazing onstage." She listed some of the productions Brooke had starred in during her short career.

"She still dances beautifully."

"I agree, but after injuries from her car accident, she couldn't keep up with the rigorous schedule being a dancer requires."

"Can you get me some information on the classes? I think my niece would love it."

"How old is she?"

"Brianna is twelve."

"There are lots of classes for her to choose from. I'll get a brochure when I'm there next week."

With less traffic, they made the trip in half the time. "I can have your tire changed in a few minutes," Omar said after he got out and came around to her side.

Morgan climbed out of the truck, unlocked her car and tossed her bag onto the backseat, then popped the trunk. She could change her own tire—her brothers had taught both her and Siobhan in case of an emergency—but rather than argue with Omar, knowing he wouldn't let her do it, she just said, "Thanks." While he worked, she leaned against his truck and studied the way his biceps flexed with each movement. Her palms itched to touch him, to run her hands over every inch of his hard body. His earlier statement came back to her, and her eyes slid closed with the remembrance.

"Morgan?"

She jerked upright. "Huh? What?"

"I called your name three times. Are you okay?" Omar

stood from his position near her front tire and closed the distance between them.

"I'm fine. Just a little worn out."

He pressed a soft kiss to her lips. "Your tire is fixed. You want me to follow you home?"

"No, that's not necessary. But I'll text you when I get home." Morgan came up on tiptoe and gave him a quick kiss. "I'll see you tomorrow."

"Can't wait to have you to myself. Night, baby." He held her door open.

"Good night." She started the car, waved and drove off. The die had been cast, and she just hoped she wouldn't come to regret this decision later.

Friday afternoon, Omar placed the last of his clothes and toiletries into the duffel bag and zipped it. His heart pounded with an excitement reminiscent of a child opening gifts on Christmas morning. He didn't know what excited him more, the certainty that he and Morgan would sleep together this weekend, or the prospect of not having to hide their growing relationship. In the mountains, away from prying eyes, he would be free to act like a man enjoying the company of his lady without worrying about either of their jobs.

After loading the truck, he locked up and headed over to pick up Morgan. When he arrived, she opened the door and gave him a smile that sent a funny feeling throughout his chest.

"Ready to get this party started?" Morgan asked.

"More ready than I've been for anything else in a long time."

"So am I." With her tone and accompanying look, he heard the message loud and clear.

She reached down for the suitcase handle, and he took the small bag. "I'll carry this for you."

She got her purse and laptop, draped a jacket over her arm and followed him out.

Omar placed her bags in the backseat, then waited for her to get in. When she climbed into the cab, he was treated to the amazing view of her shapely backside in a pair of black shorts. He gripped the door to keep from reaching for her. He'd promised not to rush her because he understood she still had some reservations about their relationship. Yet the vibes she'd been giving off said they were on the same page. With any luck, he'd be right.

"Is the traffic bad?" Morgan asked as they pulled out of the complex.

"It's getting there." Traffic was already heavy, and he anticipated a long drive ahead of them. "Might take three or four hours to get to the cabin. Did you have any problems leaving early today?"

"No. Just my nosy brother, Brandon, asking where I was going."

Omar briefly glanced her way. "What did you tell him?"

Morgan turned in her seat to face him. "Just that I was going away for the weekend. I didn't say who I was going with." She must have seen his expression because she asked, "Is that a problem?"

"I feel like a fifteen-year-old sneaking out behind my parents' backs to see the girl I like," he grumbled. "I never thought I'd have to hide out this way at twenty-eight."

"As far as my brother is concerned, I don't want him in my business. It's only for a short time. I'm not exactly thrilled about it, but I don't know any other way."

He covered her hand with his and gave it a gentle squeeze. "I know and I agree. I'll do whatever it takes to have you in my life, Morgan."

Morgan laced their fingers together. "And I'll do the same."

They shared a smile, and he refocused his attention on

the road, but didn't let go of her hand. They rode for several miles in companionable silence, with the only sounds coming from soft music flowing through the speakers. The traffic slowed, then came to a stop, and Omar looked over in time to see Morgan covering a yawn. "Tired?"

"A little," she said, leaning her head back. "I didn't get a lot sleep, and I went in to work early."

He hadn't gotten much sleep, either. Images of that sensual dance played in his head and kept him awake and aroused all night long. "Well, you should have no problems falling asleep tonight, and you can sleep in tomorrow." If he had his way, they would both get the best sleep of their lives.

It took almost four hours to reach the small town where his cabin was located, and he stopped at the local grocery store first. They were slow to emerge from the truck, and Omar stretched to loosen some of the kinks.

Morgan surveyed her surroundings. "It's beautiful. This is a nice grocery store."

"Yeah, and it's easier to shop here than trying to do it at home and having to worry about ice coolers, storage and such."

She smiled. "Ooh, you're going to cook for me again? The chili and cornbread were so good."

He slanted her an amused look, leaned against the truck and folded his arms. "No, *we* are going to cook."

"Hey, you're the resident cook with the family who owns a restaurant. And you never said what kind."

"It's a family-style restaurant—comfort foods, everybody knows everybody…like a throwback to one of those joints in the South. It's in Buena Park. We can go whenever you want."

"Are ribs on the menu?"

Omar grinned. "Fall off the bone and make you slap your mama good."

Morgan posed thoughtfully. "Hmm, I might have to break my waiting period."

He threw his head back and roared. "If that's all I need to do to be seen in public with you, we're eating there every *week*. But it won't be today, so…" He took her hand and started toward the store entrance. Inside he picked up a basket. Morgan's brows were knitted, and she was chewing on her lip. "What?"

"I'm trying to figure out a way to get out of cooking."

He chuckled. "You can't cook?"

"Yes, but I don't like to."

Omar studied her for a moment. "I'll tell you what. I brought 'Madden.' We play, and whoever loses has to cook for the whole weekend."

Her eyes lit up. *"Really?"* She rubbed her hands together with glee. "Deal. I like steak and seafood, so you'd better have a good recipe." She pulled him down an aisle. "Come on. I think I'm hungry now."

"Sweetheart, you aren't going to win, so *you'd* better dust off those cooking skills." He stopped in the meat section. "I'm partial to the porterhouse or a bone-in rib eye."

"Whatever. As long as you know how to cook it, we'll be fine."

They selected steaks and seafood and headed for the other aisles to pick up everything he thought they would need for the two-day stay. "Is there anything else you want to get? Your mint tea?"

"No, I brought some. I just want to hurry up and get to the cabin so I can beat you."

Omar chuckled. "Let's go." There was never a dull moment with Morgan.

After checking out, it only took a few minutes to reach the cabin. "I don't know what I was expecting, but this is really nice," Morgan said. The covered porch would be a great place to relax.

"Thanks. Once we get everything inside, I'll give you a tour."

"And then I can whip you at 'Madden.'"

"In your dreams. I've been playing ball since I was eight."

"So have I."

Omar just shook his head, picked up his duffel and her suitcase and headed up the steps. He opened the door, stepped back and gestured for Morgan to enter.

"This is *fabulous*," Morgan said, walking fully into the spacious living room, staring at the highly polished dark wood, floor-to-ceiling windows, stone fireplace and black leather furniture. The open design flowed seamlessly into the kitchen. "How long have you had it?"

"Only two years. I rented a cabin for a week's stay and loved it up here, so I started looking until I found this place. The owners had put it up for sale that week, and luckily I was able to top the other offers. I still paid below market value, which makes it even sweeter."

"How is it that there isn't a speck of dust anywhere?"

"There's a local woman who does housekeeping. She usually does a thorough cleaning and washes and changes the sheets when I let her know I'm coming."

"Very nice."

It took one more trip outside to bring in the groceries and store them. The kitchen boasted more wood, granite counters and stainless steel appliances, and it accessed a wraparound deck through French doors. She wouldn't have minded owning a similar spot to get away sometimes.

"Ready for the tour?"

"Yes." He showed her a large bedroom with an en suite bathroom and two smaller ones with a bathroom accessible from the hallway. Another room behind the kitchen had been set up as an entertainment room with a large TV mounted on the wall, a sophisticated stereo system and chocolate-brown leather furniture. Afterward she followed him upstairs. One half was open to downstairs and the other housed the master bedroom. "Now *this* is a master suite!" Morgan said when he opened the double doors.

Omar smiled. "I like it."

On one side of the room sat a huge bed—it had to be custom-made for his height—a walk-in closet, another wall-mounted TV and a leather bench at the foot of the bed. The other side held a pair of armchairs, a chaise lounge and another stone fireplace. She walked over to the sliding glass door. "This has to be an incredible sight at sunset," she said, staring out over the mountains and a nearby lake.

Omar fit himself behind her and slid his arms around her waist. "We can sit out and watch it if you want."

"I do." His hands roamed down to her hips, and Morgan sensed the temperature rising.

"You know, I'm supposed to get at least two kisses a day while we're here. It's after seven and I haven't gotten one." He turned her in his arms and whispered against her lips, "I need to play catch-up."

As soon as their mouths connected, she moaned. His skilled tongue stroked hers with an expertise that made every nerve in her body tingle. She ran her hands over the hard wall of his chest and wound her arms around his neck to hold him in place. Where in the world had he learned to kiss this way?

At length, he lifted his head. "There is just something about the taste of your lips. I can't get enough of kissing you." He traced his thumb across her lips, smiled and led her to the master bathroom.

The bathroom was something out of this world—a fireplace had been built into the wall behind an oversize Jacuzzi tub with steps of stone. A large window provided another spectacular view of the mountains and lake. Candles sat unlit in recesses carved into the wall and along the tub's ledge. "I need to find me a place like this. But I don't know about this window," Morgan said.

Omar laughed softly. "It's one-way. No one can see in."

"That's a relief." A vision of the two of them in the tub with the candles lit, watching the sunset, floated through her mind, and she let out an involuntary gasp.

"Morgan?"

She spun around to find him viewing her with puzzlement. She smiled brightly, hoping to distract him. No way would she tell him what she'd been thinking. "Ready for that butt-whipping?"

"The question is, are *you* ready?" he drawled.

"Let's go, Drummond." Grinning, she followed him back downstairs to the entertainment room. Morgan sincerely hoped she could keep her mind off him naked in that tub long enough to win the game.

Chapter 11

Omar turned on the television and set up the game. "Any particular team you want?"

"Doesn't matter…you pick… I'm still going to beat you. I'll let you have the Cobras since you play for them."

He stared at her in disbelief. "You sure are talking a lot of smack for someone who has never played one down in professional football."

Morgan shrugged and gestured to the game. "Quit stalling."

"Yes, ma'am. I figure we'll start with the pro level."

"Why? You scared to go all-Madden?"

His eyes widened. That was the top level where a player could control every aspect of the game. Was she *that* good? "Not at all. Whatever you want." He shrugged. "I was just trying to help you out."

She smiled. "I'm not the one who's going to need help. How about five minutes a quarter? That way you won't have to suffer too long."

Omar felt his competitive nature rise. He had planned to go easy on her but changed his mind. "Ladies first."

By halftime, he realized Morgan did, indeed, know how to play. He'd never lost one game in all the years he had played but was down by a touchdown.

At the end of the third quarter, Morgan said, "Your boys aren't doing too well, Drummond. You might need to sub some folks."

Omar frowned. "You just worry about your own team." With one minute left in the game, he'd gotten his team down to the ten-yard line. He only needed a field goal to tie, but he wanted to win. His receiver was wide-open in the end zone with the ball nearly in his hands, when out of nowhere a defender streaked across and intercepted the ball. He sat stunned as his team lost. Morgan jumped up and pumped her fists in the air.

"I am the *queen*! Say my name!"

He just stared.

She dropped back down on the sofa and sighed dramatically. "I hope you remember how I like my steak. Oh, and I'd like breakfast in bed served promptly at nine."

Her light brown eyes sparkled with laughter and as mad as he was, Omar couldn't help but smile. "You do know I'm going to want a rematch."

"Anytime, anywhere."

He shook his head. "I can't believe it."

Morgan laughed. "Aw, don't be mad. You aren't the first man I've beaten. I used to win obscene amounts of money from Malcolm's friends who figured a girl couldn't possibly know anything about football."

"You're a ringer, huh?"

"Nah. I still lose to Malcolm every now and again."

"So I have Malcolm to thank for this." He tossed the controller aside and lifted her to straddle his lap. "I'll concede to you this round, but the next one will be mine, sweet baby girl," Omar said, nuzzling her neck.

"Hmm, I'm looking forward to the challenge," she murmured.

He released the band on her hair and threaded his hands through it. "I love your hair."

Morgan reached up and fingered his locs. "I love yours, too."

He nibbled on her lush lips and teased the corners until they parted. He captured her mouth with hungry urgency. Her tongue danced and curled around his, forcing a low groan from his throat. Omar angled his head, deepened the kiss and fed himself on the sweetness of her mouth. He left her lips momentarily to trail kisses along the curve of her jaw and column of her neck. The soft fragrance she wore filtered through his senses and heightened his arousal. He kissed his way back to her mouth.

When the kiss ended, she slumped against him and laid her head on his shoulder. Both were breathing harshly, and he closed his eyes and waited for his galloping heart to slow. While he acknowledged being attracted to Morgan, the intense emotions filling him were startling and unexpected, and he needed to cool it for a minute. The lengthening shadows let him know the sun had started to go down.

"Still want to see the sunset?" he asked.

Morgan lifted her head and nodded.

Omar tucked her hair behind her ear, stood with her in his arms and carried her to the kitchen. He kissed her softly and placed her on her feet. "You might want to bring your jacket. It's gets pretty cool at night."

"Okay. I'll meet you on the deck."

His gaze followed her until she disappeared around the corner. He had placed her things in the larger downstairs bedroom, not wanting to assume anything. Omar jogged upstairs, grabbed a sweatshirt and made it back as Morgan entered the kitchen. They stepped out onto the deck, and a cool breeze greeted them.

She walked over and braced her hands on the railing. "It's so beautiful and peaceful here. I would love to have a place like this."

"Anytime you want to come up, just let me know." He wrapped her in his embrace, she placed her head on his chest and together they watched the sun dip below the horizon. He'd always enjoyed seeing the fiery colors in the sky dance across the water and slip behind the mountains, but having her here to experience it with him was a bonus. Holding her gave him a sense of peace, and he felt the places in his heart he'd closed off start to open.

Omar eased back and tilted her chin up. "You are so beautiful, smart and a hell of a 'Madden' player." He lowered his head and touched his mouth to hers. "I guess I'd better get dinner started."

"And I am hungry," Morgan said.

Inside he directed her to a bar stool and went about the task of preparing dinner. "Would you like a glass of wine?"

"Yes, please."

He retrieved the wine they'd bought earlier, which had been chilling in the wine bucket, and poured two glasses.

"Thanks. I talked to team management. They're offering a little more than your last contract, but I think we can get more."

"You think so?"

"I do. I heard some speculation that Colin won't be back at the start of the season. That might give us some leverage if it's true."

"It's true. I talked to him when I was at practice on Monday. He's thinking he won't be back until midseason." Omar decided not to share Colin's comments about Morgan being his agent.

"Wow. That just leaves Marcus because, honestly, the second-string receiver isn't that good."

He chuckled. "That's cold."

"What?" Morgan asked with a straight face. "I'm not dissing the man, just going by his numbers for the four games he started in last season."

After what he and Marcus had witnessed at practice, her assessment wasn't too far off the mark. They kept up a steady conversation about football as he cooked.

"Can I ask you a question?"

Omar turned from chopping tomatoes for the salad,

wiped his hands on a towel and came over to the bar. "What do you want to know?"

"Why did you go from wide receiver to tight end, especially with the differences in the pay scale?"

He smiled. "Did you learn that information after you became my agent or before?"

She hesitated briefly before saying, "Before."

The fact that she had been following his career made his smile widen. He wondered what she would think if she knew he'd been following *her* from the first time he'd met her at Malcolm's house two years ago. "I started out as receiver in high school and college but moved over to tight end senior year. I had hoped to go back to the receiver position, but my agent at the time was obviously just out for his cut and screwed me over. The Cobras offered to sign me at the tight end position, and I took it because I wanted to stay close to home." With his brother away in the military, Omar had wanted to be around to help Serena with the kids, especially RJ. The youngster had gone through a rebellious stage, and Omar made sure RJ stayed on the right track. He returned to the salads.

"Would you want to go back to the receiver position?"

"Definitely…unless it meant leaving home."

"I understand."

"Why?"

Morgan took a sip of her wine. "I got a call from another team."

He went still. "What did you tell them?"

"Nothing. I said thank you and I'd get back to them. But since you just said you want to stay in LA, I'll make sure you do."

He brought their plates to the table and went back for the bottle of wine. "Let's eat."

She hopped down from the stool and he held a chair out for her. "Thanks. It looks and smells great."

Omar topped off their wine and sat opposite her. He lifted his glass. "To the start of something beautiful." She gave him a shy smile and touched her glass to his. Their eyes held as they sipped. He took a moment to offer a silent blessing, and when he glanced up, he noticed she was doing the same. He waited for her to take a few bites. He had made grilled rib-eye steaks, lobster medallions, roasted herbed potatoes and a green salad. "Well?"

"I am *so* glad I won." Morgan forked up a piece of the lobster and moaned.

The soft sound coupled with the look of pure pleasure on her face sent a sharp jolt to his groin. He wasn't going to make it through the night without having her in his bed.

Morgan barely made it through dinner. Every time she looked up from her plate, she found Omar watching her. And now that they had finished, he'd been staring at her for a good two minutes as he sipped his wine, but he didn't say one word. "What are you thinking?"

Omar slowly set his glass on the table. "Truthfully?"

She nodded.

"I'm trying to figure out how I'm going to keep my word about letting you set the pace this weekend."

"And if I want the pace to be the same as yours?"

"Then we're going to *savor* every moment."

Her pulse skipped. The last time he'd used that word was at the fund-raiser. The thought of him savoring her like his favorite dessert had been on her mind since that night. This would probably be the only weekend they'd have for a while, and she wanted to make each second count.

He pushed away from the table. "Do you need anything else?"

"No, thank you. Everything was delicious." She stood and picked up her plate and glass.

"I'll clean the kitchen. Then we can relax."

Holding his gaze, Morgan said, "If I help, we can relax sooner."

Omar leaned over and kissed her. "You won't get any arguments from me."

They returned the kitchen to its former state in twenty minutes, and he led her back to the entertainment room.

"When we were at the fund-raiser, I couldn't dance with you." He picked up a remote and turned on the television, then pulled out his phone and connected it. Maxwell's smooth voice filled the room, and Omar held out his arms. "Dance with me."

He gathered Morgan in his embrace and moved to the sultry tune. They danced to song after song, each one more sensuous than the previous one. His strong hands moved up and down her back and over her hips, arousing her with each caress. He had made a playlist guaranteed to tease and seduce. By the time Jazmin Sullivan's "Let It Burn" played, her body was on fire, and she wanted to let it burn. All. Night. Long. "Omar," she whispered.

With a low growl, Omar crushed his mouth against hers.

The scorching kiss was so devastatingly erotic it weakened her knees. When she collapsed against him, he swept her into his arms and strode out of the room and up the stairs to his bedroom.

In his room, he set her on her feet and took a moment to turn on a lamp and pull the covers back on the bed. Omar came back to where Morgan stood, framed her face with his hands and kissed her tenderly. "Are you sure you're ready for this, baby? I don't want you to have any regrets, so I can wa—"

Morgan silenced him with a kiss. "You talk too much, Drummond." She reached down, pulled his shirt up and helped him remove it. "Does this answer your question?"

He answered by picking her up once again, carrying her over to the bed and stretching his tall body over hers. He peppered her face with kisses, then slid down her body, pushed her top up and kissed his way toward her breasts, taking the top with him. He came to his knees. "Sit up a minute."

She complied and he removed her top. He bent and kissed and licked his way across the portion of her breasts visible above the bra. With a flick of his wrist, he undid the clasp and dragged the straps down her arms and off. He cupped a breast in each hand, gently squeezed and massaged them, then pushed them together and circled his thumbs over her nipples. He replaced his thumbs with his tongue and kept up the exquisite torture. She cried out when he took the sensitive peaks between his teeth, and arched forward.

Omar moved back to her mouth and kissed her until she lay flat. Starting at the base of her throat, down to the valley between her breasts, he charted a path with his tongue down the front of her body, pausing to plant fleeting kisses over her belly. "This is so sexy," he said of her belly ring.

Morgan's breathing increased and she closed her eyes. Every place he touched sent sparks of pleasure coursing through her body. His hair grazed her skin, heightening the sensations. He undid her shorts and removed them and her panties, then skated his hands and tongue from her ankle to her inner thigh. She squirmed and trembled, and she called his name. No man had ever made her feel this way—treasured her like a piece of priceless art. She needed him inside her.

"Omar." Morgan reached down and tried to remove his shorts, but he shifted out of her reach. She let out a frustrated moan.

Omar chuckled. "Relax, sweetheart. We have all night. I told you, I like to savor my dessert. And *you* are a dessert of the most decadent kind."

He resumed his conquering, and a shiver passed through

her. It had been a while since her last sexual encounter, and she was already running wet and on the verge of climaxing. When he parted her slick folds and slid in a finger, an orgasm hit and nearly stole her breath. He withdrew, stood and removed the rest of his clothes. From the moment she had seen him in that commercial, Morgan knew his body would be nothing short of magnificent. And she couldn't wait to get her hands on him, especially his long, thick erection that he sheathed in a condom.

The mattress dipped beneath Omar's weight as he joined her on the bed. "I've waited a long time for you."

Before she could utter a word, he covered her mouth in an explosive kiss at the same time his fingers dipped into her center. She reached down between their bodies, grasped the base of his engorged shaft and began to stroke him.

He shuddered and let out a deep moan. "Morgan," he whispered and rested his forehead against hers.

Omar lifted his head and fixed his smoldering gaze on her. He nudged her thighs apart and eased himself inside her. He withdrew and plunged in again, filling her completely.

Morgan gasped sharply and wrapped her legs around his back. He swiveled his hips in fine, subtle, circling movements with a finesse that robbed her of all coherent thought. Waves of indescribable pleasure whipped through her, and she arched her hips up to meet the next possessive thrust. She gripped his well-developed shoulders and raked her nails down his back.

He groaned and changed the tempo, delving deeper with each rhythmic push. "I knew it would be like this between us," he panted. "You feel so good, baby."

As his strokes came faster and faster, she felt the pressure building once again. Gasping for breath, she flung her head back and convulsed in an intense orgasm. Spasms racked her body and she screamed out his name. *"Omar!"*

Omar lifted her hips higher and rode her hard through the explosive sensations, pounding into her until he found his own shattering release. He stiffened, buried his face in her neck and groaned long and low. He collapsed on the bed, half on and half off her, their ragged breathing the only sounds in the otherwise silent room. He rolled to his side, drew her into his embrace and kissed the top of her hair.

Morgan snuggled closer to him and released a satisfied sigh. She had always known that sex with Omar would be off the charts. But she hadn't expected the emotional connection—the feeling that this was more than just physical pleasure. Choosing not to dwell on those thoughts, she wrapped an arm around his midsection and closed her eyes. Her body still hummed with passionate aftershocks, and she drifted off with a smile.

She awakened in Omar's arms as he carried her across the room.

"Where are we going?" she asked, her body already responding to the heat of his naked body.

"To the Jacuzzi."

The electric fireplace and candles provided the only light in the otherwise darkened bathroom. He walked up the three stairs, stepped into the tub and placed her on her feet. He sat and pulled her to sit in front of him. She braided her hair and coiled it into a loose bun to keep it from getting wet.

"Is the water okay?"

She leaned against his wide chest and sighed contentedly. "Mmm." Outside, the moon and millions of stars shone in the midnight sky. She couldn't think of anything more perfect. She gasped softly when Omar's caresses began again. Turning, she straddled his muscular thighs, kissed him and ground her body against his.

Omar groaned. "Don't start something you don't plan to finish."

"Oh, I plan to do more than finish, baby." Morgan reached beneath the water and grasped his condom-sheathed erection. "And you're all ready for me."

"I'm more than ready for you, sweetheart."

He lifted her and brought her down slowly, inch by exquisite inch. They both moaned. On second thought, she could think of one more thing to make this night perfect.

Chapter 12

Still trying to sleep, Morgan swiped at something brushing her cheek and flipped over in bed.

Omar chuckled. "Wake up, sleepyhead."

"Go away," she murmured.

"If I go away, you won't get your breakfast in bed."

She turned, slowly opened her eyes and squinted in the bright sunlight streaming through the now-open drapes. Omar stood next to the bed wearing a sleeveless tee, basketball shorts and a wide grin. "Breakfast?"

He nodded. "You said nine o'clock."

"It's nine already? I feel like I've been asleep for only three or four hours."

Desire filled his eyes, and his voice dropped an octave. "That's because you kept me up all night."

Her nipples tightened and her core throbbed. After making love in the bathtub, they'd slept for a short time before he woke her up and they began again. The man possessed an incredible amount of stamina.

"If you keep looking at me like that," he said, "I'm the only one who'll be eating breakfast this morning."

Morgan's pulse skipped. "I... I need to go to the bathroom first." It dawned on her that her bag was in the downstairs bedroom. "My bag—"

Omar gestured to the bench at the foot of the bed. "I brought it up."

"Thanks." She made a move to get up but remembered she didn't have anything on.

"What's wrong?"

"I need something to put on."

He lifted an eyebrow. "Please don't tell me you're all shy now…not after everything we did last night and this morning."

Heat stung her face.

"I'll go get breakfast." Smiling, he tossed her a wink and left the room.

As soon as the door closed, she hopped up, grabbed her stuff out of the bag and went into the bathroom. By the time he came back, she was dressed and sitting up in bed. He had such a look of displeasure on his face, she asked, "What?"

"The jersey. You can wear my number."

Morgan laughed. She had on a football jersey with Malcolm's name and number. "You are such a man. And I cannot wear your jersey."

"You can wear it around the house…for now."

"Pitiful. Fine, I'll wear it around the house." The smile that bloomed on his face made her shake her head.

He placed the tray across her lap, came around to the other side of the bed and carefully climbed in next to her.

"This looks good. Thank you." Morgan rarely took the opportunity to cook a large breakfast for herself. She typically ate on the run. But this sexy man had prepared a feast—eggs, grits, bacon, biscuits, fruit and her favorite mint tea—and she planned to enjoy every bite. His plate was on the tray, as well. She scooted closer so they could share. While eating, she decided to ask the question that had been bugging her. "Last night you said something about waiting for me for a long time. What did you mean?"

Omar placed the fork on his plate and took a sip of his coffee before answering. "Just what I said. I wanted you the first time I saw you at Malcolm's house two years ago. You had on a thin-strapped purple dress that stopped a few inches above your knees and gold-colored sandals, and your hair was pulled back in a ponytail. And your smile… I thought you were the most beautiful woman I'd ever seen. I couldn't stop looking at you."

She was amazed that he had paid so much attention to her and impressed that he'd remembered what she had worn two years ago. "You never said anything other than a few words to me, and all of our conversations have been casual."

"You were dating someone."

She frowned at the remembrance.

"He was a basketball player—Jabari Mitchell—right? What happened?"

"Yeah, but we broke up not long afterward. He seemed to think I'd be okay with him sleeping around while he was on the road, just as long as he came home to me."

"His loss, my gain."

"So, why now as opposed to then?"

"You're not the only one who's had relationship problems," Omar answered and popped a piece of bacon in his mouth.

Morgan recalled some rumors surrounding him and a woman, but being embroiled in her own drama, she hadn't had time to be concerned about his. However, she was curious now. "Is it something you can tell me about?" He seemed uncomfortable, so she added, "If it's too—"

"No, no, it's fine." He blew out a long breath. "The woman I was dating decided she wanted to take our relationship to reality TV and went so far as to sign a contract and forge my name."

She stared. "How did she think she could get away with something like that?"

He shrugged. "I have no idea. I guess she thought she could convince me to do the show. It wasn't until someone from the network called me talking about how happy they were to be working with me, and giving me production dates, that I even had a clue about what was going on. I found out later she'd practiced copying my signature from an autograph I signed, supposedly for one of her friend's kids. It was crazy. She figured she could use my name to get her fifteen minutes of fame."

"What about your agent?"

Omar snorted. "That idiot wouldn't return my calls, and when he finally did, he tried to convince me the show would be good for my image. The only thing he was interested in was getting a large piece of the pie. Hell, if I had done that show, there would've been nothing left of my image. And there was no way I'd agree to have my relationships played out for the world to see—my parents, my brother's family and my personal life." He shook his head. "They tried to hold me to the contract, but I threatened to sue her, the network and my agent, and they dropped it."

Morgan didn't know what to say. Between what he had just told her, what she knew about his first agent and now Roland, it was no wonder he wanted to steer clear of anyone connected to the league. "I'm sorry."

"So was I."

"Did you love her?"

He lifted his eyes to meet hers. "I thought I did, but when I didn't feel anything but anger and could easily dismiss her, I realized it wasn't love. What about you?"

"We hadn't dated long enough to say it was love, but after having everybody in my business and feeling like a fool, I promised myself I'd never date another athlete."

"Not all athletes are like that." He stroked a finger down her cheek. "*I'm* not like that."

Their eyes held. "That's good to know." She picked up her fork again, and they finished eating in companionable silence.

"After I clean up, we can take a walk to the lake."

"I'd like that." She thought about offering to help with the dishes, but she wanted some time to think. She hadn't planned to reveal all that, especially the part about not dating someone in the sports field. He said he wouldn't treat her like Jabari had and she wanted to believe him because, despite her vow, she was falling for him.

Omar started the dishwasher, braced his hands on the counter and bowed his head. Talking about the mess with Latrice had stirred up all the anger and mistrust all over again. It had taken him more than a year after that fiasco to go out on a date, and those few had been nothing more than casual outings. But this thing with Morgan had gone way beyond casual. If he had any doubts about how serious things were, he only had to go back to the fact that he'd invited her into his private space. No one outside his family had been here, and very few people even knew about the place. Then there was last night's lovemaking. On some level, he had known it would be incredible, but he never expected the depths of emotion that had nearly consumed him. Just thinking about the way she called his name and her rapturous expression when she climaxed made him hard all over again. Omar sucked in a deep breath.

"Omar?"

He spun around. "Hey, baby."

Morgan's brows knitted together. "Are you all right?"

"Yeah, just thinking about some stuff." His thoughts were solely on getting her in his bed again. "You ready to go?"

She nodded. "What's the weather like?"

"Supposed to get up to eighty-one, but it's already seventy-six." She had changed into a snug-fitting tee and a pair of white cropped pants.

"Okay. Then I won't need a jacket."

"No. Let me grab my shoes and keys and we can go."

After returning, he led her through the back gate at the far edge of his property. He reached for her hand, and they strolled down the path leading to the lake. Several other people obviously had the same idea to take advantage of the nice summer weather. He found a spot for the two of them to view the water, pulled Morgan to stand in front of him and loosely draped his arms around her waist. She glanced up at him, smiled and covered his hands with hers, then turned back toward the water. Omar kissed the top of her hair and tightened his hold. If not for football season, he would have brought her up here every weekend just so they could be together openly. He didn't know how he was going to manage the business-only facade once they returned home. And he didn't want to. But trying to convince her they could make it work would be an uphill battle, and one he didn't think he'd win. He sighed inwardly. Rather than risk the chance of her erecting her professional walls again, he'd just have to wait it out. It was only a few weeks.

"I love it here," Morgan said after a long while. "It would be nice to come up again."

"I was thinking the same thing. But with the season starting in a couple of weeks, I won't be able to do it until the bye week."

"Yeah, and by then it'll probably be too cold."

"We could always snuggle up in the cabin in front of the fireplace. And I promise you won't feel cold for one minute." Omar trailed kisses along her jaw and whispered close to her ear just how he planned to keep her warm. He heard her sharp intake of breath and felt her tremble. She turned in his arms and, before he could stop himself, his lips were on hers.

After a few short seconds, Morgan tore her mouth away and buried her head in his chest. They both were breathing harshly. "We're standing in the middle of a crowded area, Drummond."

"True, but none of them know us."

"That's not what I mean."

He leaned back and stared at her for a moment. "Are you saying you're embarrassed?"

"Something like that," she murmured. "A peck here and there is fine, but the whole lip-lock thing…"

Omar chuckled. "I get it. Then we'll save the heavy stuff for when we get back to the cabin." He took her hand and started off farther down the path. "I thought we'd go out to dinner tonight."

"Sounds good. I had no idea there were so many shops here. I was expecting to find a more rural place."

"We'll eat at one of the restaurants in Big Bear Lake Village. They have all kinds of restaurants and shops, a movie theater, a bank and bowling."

"I can't wait."

They walked awhile longer, stopped at one of the eateries for lunch and then retraced their steps back to his cabin.

"You mind if I do a little work?" Morgan asked.

"Of course not. If you'd like to work on the deck, I'll move the furniture outside." Omar typically stored all the furniture in the garage or small shed he'd had built to protect it from the weather.

"That would be great. Thanks." She gave him one of her beautiful smiles, came up on tiptoe to kiss his cheek and walked out.

He smiled and went to the shed. *Yep, I like her a lot.* By the time she returned, he had pulled out two loungers, wiped them down and covered them with the cushions he'd removed from their plastic bags. He'd also set up a small table.

Morgan sat on one of the loungers and removed several manila folders from her bag. "What are you going to be doing?"

"Probably research some psychology programs."

"Cool. You can join me out here."

He retrieved his laptop and took the other lounger. In between his searches, he stole glances at Morgan as she pored over some photos. He studied her rotating a particular picture one way first, then another while frowning. Omar refocused his attention on the computer screen. He didn't know how much time passed before he looked up to find her frowning again and typing on her phone. "Something wrong?"

She turned her head in his direction. "Just going over the pictures from a case I'm handling at work and sending an email."

"I read about the lawsuit."

Morgan released a deep sigh. "I don't know why my father decided to make this my first case."

"Maybe because he sees the same thing I do—a beautiful, intelligent woman who can handle anything thrown her way."

"Thanks. How's your search going?"

"Not too bad. I found a few colleges that offer distance learning programs. That's the only way I'll be able to juggle school with football, and even then, it won't be easy."

"No, but I'm confident you'll be able to do both very well."

"I appreciate the vote of confidence." They shared a smile and went back to their respective tasks. Morgan was the first woman he'd dated who didn't need to fill every moment with conversation, and he found himself enjoying the easy rapport they were building.

Two hours later, he'd made notes on four prospective schools. He shut down his computer, crossed the short distance and sat on the edge of Morgan's lounger. "How much longer do you plan to work?"

"I can stop whenever. What time are we going to dinner?"

"I made reservations for six, but I wanted to go a little earlier so you have a chance to see some of the village shops."

"I didn't bring anything dressy."

"You don't need to dress up. If you have a pair of long pants, I'd wear them because it'll be much cooler when we come back." He stood.

Morgan rubbed her arms. "The temperatures are already starting to cool." She put everything back into her folders, and Omar helped her up. "It's four o'clock now. I can be ready in half an hour. I want to take a quick shower."

Omar wiggled his eyebrows. "We can shower together and save time."

She laughed. "Save time? *Right*. Mmm-hmm, and we won't make that six-o'clock reservation."

He placed his hand over his heart. "You doubt my intentions?"

She poked him in the chest. "You can cut the innocent act, Drummond." She pressed her body close to his and slid her arms around his waist. "But we can shower together later."

The feel of her so snugly against him tested his control, and he groaned. "You can't just rub your body against me like this and leave me hanging."

"I'm not leaving you hanging. I said *later*." Morgan dropped her arms, picked up her belongings and went inside. She paused. "You coming?"

"Yeah," he grumbled and followed her in and upstairs to his bedroom.

She gathered her clothes and went into the bathroom.

Rather than wait, he used one of the downstairs bathrooms to shower. Afterward he tied a towel around his waist and went back to his bedroom for clothes.

"Well, well," Morgan said, coming out of the bathroom. "See something you like, Ms. Gray?"

"As a matter of fact, I do. Liked it from the moment I saw you on that commercial."

Omar chuckled.

"Wondered what was beneath the towel, too."

His hands went to the towel. "I'll be glad to give you a private show."

"We're going to be late."

"Yes, we are." He dropped the towel, closed the distance between them and covered her mouth in a hungry kiss. "Very late," he murmured against her lips while undoing the buttons on her top. In his estimation, they might not make dinner at all.

Chapter 13

They finally made it to dinner two hours later. Morgan stared at the pleased look on Omar's face over the rim of her glass. "You really need to practice a little self-control."

"*Me?* I'm not the one who was talking about wanting to see what was beneath the towel."

"Yeah, you. You're the one going around tempting folks, wearing nothing but that towel." The moment she'd seen him, visions of him naked and straddling her body rushed back to her, and she hadn't cared one iota about dinner. Only him.

"For your information, I have a lot of self-control. If I didn't, we wouldn't be sitting in this nice restaurant." Omar lifted his glass in mock toast and took a sip of his lemonade.

The upscale restaurant, with its dim lighting, soft music and candles, was perfect for lovers. The weekend had been magical and she wasn't ready for it to end, but tomorrow they would have to go back to the real world. After two days of being openly affectionate, it was going to be hard to pretend otherwise the next time they saw each other in public.

As if reading her thoughts, he reached across the table and grasped her hand. "I don't know how I'm going to be able to go back to keeping us a secret, Morgan."

"Me, either, but…" She trailed off, and her eyes pleaded with him to understand.

"I know, baby. We'll make it work." He gave her hand a reassuring squeeze. "Let's just enjoy ourselves and deal with the rest later."

"Okay." They dined on excellently prepared crab-stuffed salmon, seasoned rice and sautéed vegetables while laughing and talking.

When they were done, Omar asked, "Do you want something else, more tea?"

"Maybe some dessert to go." Morgan picked up the menu the hostess had left and viewed the selections. "Are you getting something?"

"I haven't decided. Although I didn't eat too badly during the off season, I need to get my eating back on track. But this Grand Finale Chocolate Cake looks good."

"It does." The three-layer dark chocolate cake with chocolate frosting would be the perfect end to the meal. "If we share a slice, we can cut our calories in half."

"I like the way you think." He ordered the cake to go and settled the bill, and they strolled hand in hand back to the truck.

They spent the evening enjoying the dessert, watching movies, laughing and making love. It was as if they both knew this would have to sustain them for a while. Omar made love to her with a tenderness that brought tears to Morgan's eyes, and she fell a little harder.

The next morning, she helped him pack up the leftover food and supplies they'd brought and close up the house. She took one last look around, letting the memories fill her heart, and followed him out to the truck.

Omar started the engine and drove them to the gas station. He filled the tank and got them on the road. "As soon as our schedules permit, we'll plan another trip, though it might not be until the first of next year."

She didn't see that happening until the football season ended, and he implied they would still be together. She tried not to think about the future because there was no guarantee their relationship would last that long. Omar had said he would be faithful, but then, so did Jabari in the beginning. Watching the passing scenery, she decided to focus on the here and now.

"Do you have a busy week?" Omar asked a while later when they stopped for lunch.

"I do. Between a couple of important meetings at work and getting ready for the dance show and reception on Friday, it's going to be crazy."

"Brooke mentioned it being a fund-raiser."

"Yes. She wants to be able to offer classes to more students, especially those who can't afford it. The money will go to hiring instructors and expanding the studio. The building next door became vacant a month ago, and Brooke wants to make an offer before someone else does."

"Don't forget to get me a brochure for my niece." They disposed of their trash and got back on the road.

"I won't," Morgan said, continuing their conversation. "I'll get it Monday night and drop it off to you on Tuesday during my lunch."

"I'll be at the practice facility. Can you come there or do you want me to meet you somewhere?"

"No, it's fine. Might be a good time for a face-to-face introduction with management anyway." Up to this point, everything had been conducted through email, but seeing them in person would make it real. "Are you starting practice early?"

"Nah. Going to help out some of the newer guys."

"Any competition I need to be worried about?"

Omar looked offended. "Competition? For my job? Please."

Morgan rolled her eyes. "Oh, silly me. Forget I asked."

"That's right."

"Be careful that your head doesn't explode from being so full of yourself," she said with a laugh.

"I'm not foolish enough to believe that someone won't

come along who is better than me, but for now…" He shrugged.

"Just drive, Drummond."

His laughter filled the truck's interior.

They lapsed into a comfortable silence, and Morgan dosed off. When she awakened they were about ten miles from home. She stretched. "Wow, I didn't realize I slept that long. Sorry."

"No problem. You must have been tired."

"Well, I didn't get much rest this weekend, thanks to you," she said, trying to hide her smile.

Omar opened his mouth to answer, but his cell rang. He engaged the vehicle's Bluetooth. "Hello?"

"Omar, it's Serena. Something happened with Rashad and he took off. He just snapped and left. I've never seen him like this." His sister-in-law's frantic voice came through the speakers.

"Slow down and tell me what happened," he said calmly.

"I don't know. We were sitting in the family room watching TV, and all of a sudden he bolted upright in the chair and started shaking."

"What was on the television?"

"Baseball highlights, I think."

"Where were the kids?"

"Brianna was in the kitchen cooking, and RJ was in his room. I went over to the trailer and tried to talk to him, but he wouldn't open the door." She started to cry.

He scrubbed a hand down his face. "Don't cry, sis. I'll go by and try to talk to him."

"Thank you. I'm sorry for interrupting your day."

"You're not interrupting my day. After I check on him, I'll be over. Hang in there, Serena."

When Omar ended the call, Morgan ran a comforting hand down his arm.

"Do you mind if I stop to check on my brother first? I just need to make sure he's okay."

"Of course not." She felt her own emotions rising and couldn't imagine what Serena was going through. Her father had been one of the fortunate ones who didn't show any lasting effects of his time in combat, but she remembered hearing her parents talking about Uncle Thad's struggles. She glanced over at Omar, and her admiration for him went up another notch.

Omar tried to keep his emotions in check but had a difficult time. Rashad hadn't had an episode like this in a while, and Omar hoped this wasn't a sign of regression. The Sunday congestion on the freeway didn't help his mood, and by the time he pulled into the trailer park, he was a wreck. He reminded himself that he couldn't help Rashad in his current state and drew in several calming breaths.

Morgan grasped his hand. "It would be better if I waited out here."

"Yes. I appreciate your understanding." He brought her hand to his lips and placed a lingering kiss on the back.

"I'll be saying a little prayer that he's okay."

"Thanks." He got out, crossed to the trailer and knocked on the door. When there was no answer, he stuck his key in the lock and entered cautiously. "Rashad, it's me." He rounded the corner and stopped short at the sight of his brother sitting on the floor against the sofa, knees to his chest, arms wrapped tightly around his legs, with his head bowed. Omar eased himself to the floor a short distance away and waited.

After about twenty minutes, Rashad finally looked up. "Serena call you?"

He nodded.

"She upset?"

"She's concerned, yes. Want to talk about it?"

Several minutes passed before Rashad spoke again. "It was the smell…reminded me of burning flesh."

Omar frowned. "What was the smell?"

"Eggs…eggs."

He remembered Serena mentioning Brianna was cooking and wondered if she had burned them. "Did you say anything to Serena about it?"

"No. My hands started shaking, my heart was pounding and I couldn't breathe. Do you have any idea how that made me feel, to have my wife see me that way? I'm supposed to take care of her, not the other way around. And my kids…what kind of man can't be there for his kids?"

"You're supposed to take care of each other, bro. It's a partnership. And you are there for Bri and RJ. Are there any other smells you know of that trigger the response?"

He rattled off a list of four other things. "But when I know Serena is cooking those foods, I go outside until it's ready. I never know when the other things will set me off."

"Don't you think she'd stop cooking them or at least let you know they're on the stove if you told her? Rashad, Serena isn't a mind reader, and she loves you, man."

"I know, and I love her more than my own life," he said emotionally. "I just can't… I don't know how to…"

Omar scooted closer and placed a hand on Rashad's shoulder. "You don't need all the answers today. Start with one step at a time, like calling Serena to let her know you're okay," he suggested gently. "If you're up to it, maybe explain what happened and share with her what you told me." They talked awhile longer about what Rashad wanted to tell Serena.

Rashad nodded. "Yeah, okay. But I don't have my phone. Since I left without saying anything and wouldn't open the door when she came by, do you think she'll talk to me?"

He handed over his cell. "I *know* she'll talk to you. I'll bet she's just waiting for your call." He rose to his feet. "I'll go outside until you're done."

Morgan glanced up at his approach. He opened her door and leaned against the frame. "Sorry it's taking so long." He had been inside for close to an hour.

"It's no problem. This is important. Is he okay?" Her concerned gaze searched his face.

"As much as he can be right now. I convinced him to call Serena. He's using my phone, so when he's done I'll drive you home."

"Take your time, baby."

Omar bent and placed a tender kiss on her lips. He didn't have the words to describe how much her support meant to him. And hearing her call him *baby*... All the places in his heart that he'd purposely closed off were starting to open, one room at a time.

"I think your brother is finished," she said.

He turned to find Rashad standing outside his door with a questioning look. "Hang on." He walked over and took the phone in his brother's outstretched hand.

"You didn't tell me you were with someone," Rashad said. "Who is she?"

"Morgan Gray."

Rashad's eyebrows shot up. "Your agent?" At Omar's nod, he added, "And your new woman."

"Yeah. We were on our way back from the cabin when Serena called."

A look of panic crossed Rashad's face. "Does she know?"

Omar didn't want to lie to his brother. "Yes, but she understands. Her father and uncle are veterans. I would like for you to meet her."

"Okay. But not today, though."

He turned toward the truck and Morgan smiled. "Whenever you're ready."

"She looks too pretty to be running around with a bunch of football players. You sure she knows what she's doing?"

He thought back to how she had beaten him at "Madden," and Marcus's comments. "Believe me, she knows the game. Are you going home today?"

"Yeah, but I think I need a little more time. And I told Serena about the other stuff."

"I'm proud of you." They shared a rough embrace. "You're my hero. Always will be," Omar said with emotion clogging his throat. "I'll see you later." Now that he knew some of the triggers, he and Serena could figure out ways to help minimize Rashad's exposure. He climbed into the truck, and Morgan laid a hand on his arm.

"How are you doing?" Morgan asked.

"I'm good now." His brother seemed to be making baby steps toward healing, and he just spent forty-eight hours with an incredible woman. Yeah, he was good. It took another twenty-five minutes to reach Morgan's condo, and he was reluctant to end their time. He carried her bags to the door and set them inside.

Morgan faced him. "Thank you so much for the weekend. I really enjoyed myself, especially breakfast in bed for two days," she added with a sly grin.

"Well, rest assured, next time *you'll* be doing the cooking." Omar drew her into his arms. "I enjoyed this weekend, too. I'm going to have a hard time keeping my hands off you the next time I see you." He leaned down and captured her mouth in a long, drugging kiss. "I gotta go, sweetheart."

"Be safe and let me know how Serena is doing."

"I will." He kissed her once more, then headed back to his truck.

Serena was waiting when Omar arrived and greeted

him with a strong hug. "I don't know how to thank you for always being here for us," she said with tears in her eyes.

"No thanks needed. We're family, and that's what families do."

She wiped away the tears and led him into the house.

"Where are Bri and RJ?"

"They're in their rooms. I wanted to talk to you for a few minutes first."

He followed her to the kitchen and straddled a chair.

"You want something to eat or drink?"

"No, thanks. I ate earlier. What's up?"

"Now that I know some of the things that cause flashbacks for Rashad, what do I do now? I mean, aside from making sure I warn him or change some of the foods I cook."

"I plan to talk to one of the psychologists who will be on staff at the center for a few ideas. I'm just glad he's beginning to open up."

"So am I. If it wasn't for you, I don't think he would have. Mom and Dad are going to be so happy when I tell them. He said he'd be home by dinner. You're welcome to stay."

"Not tonight. I'm just coming back from the cabin, and I want to get home and relax."

"Isn't that what you typically do when you're there?"

Omar nodded. His mind went back to his time with Morgan—the walk along the lake, watching the sunset, their incredible lovemaking. His body reacted just thinking about the pleasure they shared.

"Then why—?" Serena studied him critically, then smiled. "Ooh-wee, things are moving fast with your lady agent."

"How do you know…?" He trailed off at the look on her face. "Yes."

"I knew it! You can't fool me. She seems like a nice person."

"She is, and I really like her. But you have to keep this to yourself for a while." After this weekend, he wanted the world to know about him and Morgan, but he promised not to say anything.

Serena walked over to a trio of round wicker baskets mounted on the wall, got some potatoes and took them to the sink. She angled her head and placed a hand on her hip. "Why? She's not involved in anything shady, is she?"

He laughed. "No. She just doesn't want it to get out that she's dating her first client."

"I can see that. The first thing folks would say is that she slept her way to the top."

"Exactly. I couldn't care less what anybody thinks, but I won't do anything to ruin this opportunity for her."

"Sounds like my baby brother is falling in love."

His reply was preempted by RJ's appearance.

"Hey, Uncle O. I didn't know you were here." RJ adjusted his glasses and walked straight to the refrigerator and got the carton of juice.

"What's up, little man?"

"Not much. Are you still taking us to lunch this week?" he asked, reaching into the cabinet for a cup.

"That's the plan. Most likely on Wednesday, if it's all right with your mom."

"Mom?"

"Fine with me."

"Yes!" RJ pumped his fists in the air, set the cup on the counter and ran out of the room yelling for his sister, who came barreling into the kitchen.

Brianna wrapped her slender arms around his neck. "Hi, Uncle Omar."

"Hey, baby girl." He chatted with the children for a few minutes and said his goodbyes.

When Omar arrived home, he was struck by the silence that greeted him. After two days of waking up next to Morgan, he was not looking forward to spending the night alone. Somehow he had to find a way to get her back in his arms. And sooner rather than later.

Chapter 14

Morgan's smile was still in place Monday morning when she arrived at her office. She passed her assistant and called out a cheery "Good morning, Evelyn," but didn't break stride. Seated behind her desk, she booted up the computer and went through her emails. Her heart began to race when she saw one from John Bledsoe with the preliminary results from the tests run on the rail. She clicked on the message and quickly read. From what she could see, the rail was structurally sound, and there was no reason for it to come away from the wall. *Then why?* She read further and frowned.

She picked up the phone and called Brandon to see if he had a minute to talk.

"Sure. Come on over."

"Be there in a minute." Morgan hung up, printed out the email, grabbed the folder containing the photographs she'd taken of the rail and headed to his office.

"What's going on, sis?" Brandon asked when she entered.

"John sent the preliminary findings on the rail." She handed him the email. "Pay attention to the second paragraph."

His brow lifted, and he angled his head in her direction. "Sticky substance on the ends?"

"The only substance that should have been on the ends was the glue we provide in the kit. And it doesn't look like that. I noticed it on a couple of the pictures I took." She handed them over and pointed out the area. The glue was specially formulated to adhere to tile, granite and other bathroom materials, and also acted as a seal.

"Is this saying they used a different type of glue?"

She shrugged. "We won't know exactly what it is until the tests are complete. But it does bring up a few questions."

Brandon drummed his fingers on the desk. "And makes me wonder what else Porter is trying to hide."

"Yeah, me, too. Which is why I'll be going over each photo and every scrap of paper with a fine-tooth comb."

"Are you staying late tonight? If you are, let me know so I can hang out until you leave."

"I have a dance class tonight, so I'm leaving on time, if not a few minutes early. Are you guys ready to do your dance on Friday?"

"Of course. When we get done, there are going to be so many checks written that Brooke is gonna make us part of her annual show permanently." He stood and did a little dance step, ending with a spin.

Morgan rolled her eyes and walked toward the door. "That's my cue."

Laughing, he said, "Keep me posted."

"I will." She shook her head. She liked seeing this playful side of Brandon and wished he would relax and behave this way more often. All of her brothers were intense, but he took it to new heights. Even Khalil, who was the most serious of the bunch, made time for fun.

She stopped short upon seeing Evelyn in her office when she returned. "Evelyn?" Morgan swore the woman jumped ten feet in the air.

"Oh, I was just putting two messages on your desk." Evelyn skirted around Morgan and rushed out.

She took a cursory glance around her desk to see if something had been moved or was missing but didn't notice anything. Setting aside the puzzling encounter, she

sent a message to John asking him to email or call as soon
as the test results came in, and then she went through the
photographs again. She had no idea what she was looking for but figured she'd know it when she saw it. Morgan
tagged a few questionable ones that she planned to inspect further and made more notes. By the time she looked
up, she had worked way past lunchtime, and her stomach
had begun to lodge a protest by growling so loudly that it
startled her. She stood, stretched and grabbed her wallet.

"Evelyn, I'm going down to the café. I'll be right back."

"Enjoy yourself."

Morgan paused briefly and stared. *Why is she being so
nice all of a sudden?* Maybe the woman had taken Morgan's threat to report her seriously. Whatever the case, it
was a welcome change. Shaking her head, she continued to
her destination. Twenty minutes later, she dropped down in
her chair, unwrapped the turkey sandwich and took a huge
bite. Paired with a cup of chicken noodle soup, it should
hold her until she made it home after dance class tonight.
Morgan rotated her chair toward the window.

With nothing to occupy her mind at the moment, her
thoughts automatically traveled to the weekend with Omar.
She had enjoyed every second of the trip, and her body
heated up just thinking about the man's bedroom skills.
And that passionate encounter in the tub… Her eyes drifted
closed as every vivid detail came rushing back—from his
caresses and kisses to the way she had ridden him in the
candlelit space with the moon streaming through the window, bringing her to climax after climax and making her
scream his name.

"Ms. Gray?"

Morgan jerked upright, spun around in her chair and
placed the forgotten sandwich on her desk. "Yes."

"You have a phone call on line two."

"Thank you." She'd been so lost in her memories that

she hadn't ever heard the phone ring. She picked up the receiver. "Morgan Gray."

"Good afternoon, sweetheart," came the warm baritone.

She gripped the phone tighter. Just the sound of his voice turned her on. "Hey, yourself. What's up?"

"Just missing you and wanting to hear your lovely voice."

"I miss you, too," she murmured.

"I have to tell you, I didn't sleep too well last night."

Neither had she, but she wasn't going to tell him. "Poor baby," she teased. "Maybe a nice, hot cup of mint tea will help. It always does the trick for me. It's very soothing."

"I don't think the mint tea will work. The only thing that can help me is another dose of you."

Morgan almost dropped the receiver.

"I can't wait to sample your sweetness again. This time I think I'll conduct a *thorough* taste test. I don't want to miss one spot. Would you like that?"

Her body trembled, and an ache started in her core. *Yes and now!* "Yes," she whispered. "Do...do I get to do a taste test? I'm going to start at your sexy lips, work my way over your strong jaw and down to your amazing chest. Mmm, I might have to linger there for a bit. I don't want to miss one spot," she added, using his words. "Then I'm going to—"

"Morgan, baby," Omar said, his voice strained. "If you keep talking, I am going to be at your office in thirty minutes. And I'm *not* coming to talk."

She immediately snapped her mouth shut. What was she thinking? Her gaze darted to the door, and she breathed a sigh of relief upon seeing that it was closed. "Um... I need to get back to work."

"Yeah, and I need to go take a cold shower."

"It's your fault. You started it," Morgan fussed, but she was smiling.

"And when I see you next, I'm going to finish it."

"I don't think so. The next time we meet will be tomorrow at the Cobras practice facility, and you will have your professional hat on." He grumbled something about what she could do with that hat, and she laughed.

"Ha-ha, funny. I'll see you tomorrow."

"Okay," he said.

She was still chuckling when she hung up. She picked up her spoon, finished her lunch and grabbed another file.

Morgan worked steadily for the next hour, then packed up to leave. She met Siobhan coming down the hallway. "You still here?" Morgan observed.

"Not for long. Justin and I are going out to dinner, so we're heading straight there. How was your weekend?"

She felt a rush of heat on her face.

Siobhan smiled. "That good, huh? I take it you took Omar up on his offer."

"I did."

"Well, I'm glad you had a good time. I hope you remember what I told you. See you later."

Yes, she remembered that Siobhan had told her to be careful of falling for him. And yes, Morgan was afraid she might have been right. Sighing, she took the elevator down to the parking garage and got into her car. It took almost an hour to reach the studio, and Brooke was waiting in the office with a big smile on her face.

"So, any updates on your budding romance?"

"Hello to you, too, Brooke."

"Hi. Well? Don't keep me in suspense. I know something happened after last week, especially with the way he was looking at you. Since I'm not getting any action, I have to live vicariously through you."

Morgan dropped her bag on a chair and folded her arms. "Whatever, girl. You get plenty of action. But to answer your question, we spent the weekend at his mountain cabin."

Brooke's eyes widened and her mouth fell open.

Morgan reached over and pushed her chin up. "Close your mouth before something flies in."

"I mean, I was expecting you to tell me something like you shared a few steamy kisses, but...*wow*. You two aren't wasting any time. I guess you're doing a little more than just 'seeing him casually,'" Brooke said, making quote marks in the air.

"He's... I don't know...different, smart, caring, loyal. I didn't expect to like him this much." She had sensed a shift in their relationship the last time they made love. It was gentle and stirred her deeper emotions.

"If he has all those great qualities, it should work out fine, because you're the same way." She glanced over to the open door and lowered her voice conspiratorially. "Is he good in bed?"

Morgan couldn't stop the smile spreading across her lips. *"Incredible."*

Brooke squealed and slapped a hand over her mouth. "I knew it. I wouldn't expect anything less from a man who looks like that." She fanned herself. "I think I'm going to start watching football more often. You can get me a ticket to a game, right?"

Morgan burst out laughing. "Yeah, I'm sure I can talk to Malcolm about it."

"Are there any others on the team who look that good?"

"Quite a few."

"Okay. Count me in for at least one game."

"I've invited you to Malcolm's barbecues, but you always decline."

"I won't be declining the next one," Brooke said with a straight face and strutted out of the room.

Morgan smiled. True, there were some good-looking guys on the team, but in her mind, none of them held a candle to Omar Drummond on or off the field.

* * *

Tuesday afternoon, Omar jogged over to the sideline to get a drink. He had planned to do only a couple of drills with a rookie tight end, but somehow got roped into a speed and agility workout. He checked his phone and saw that Morgan had left him a text letting him know she'd be arriving around one. He had a good thirty minutes, which gave him time to take a quick shower.

On his way back to the field, a woman called out to him. He turned and released a deep sigh. "Hey, Andrea."

"Well, hello, stranger. Long time no see. How've you been?"

"Good, and you?"

"I'd be better if you took me up on my offer."

"Sorry, but the answer is still the same." Andrea Fletcher was one of the team's cheerleaders and, although there was nothing specific written in the rules, every player knew they were off limits. It kept the drama to a minimum. And even if they weren't, she'd never make the list of women he would date. She had a killer body with everything in the right places, and a beautiful mocha face, but she reminded him of his ex—high-maintenance. She had been trying to get him to go out with her for the past two years, and he'd turned her down every time. He figured after the last time, she had finally gotten the hint and moved on. Apparently not. And as quiet as it was kept, she had dated at least three players on the team, moving on to the next when one was cut from the team or demoted to second or third string. She moved closer, and he took a step back.

"I know you're a stickler for the *unwritten* rule about not dating the cheerleaders on the team, but I have great news. I just turned in my resignation because I scored a spot in a dance production."

"Congratulations. I wish you the best."

"Now that I'm not affiliated with the team, we can be

free to date." Andrea slid her arms around his waist and said sultrily, "And I promise you won't regret it for one minute."

She leaned up and tried to kiss him, and he averted his head. "The answer is still no." Omar gently but firmly removed her arms and looked up. His gaze connected with Morgan's furious one. He cursed under his breath.

"Hello, Mr. Drummond. I'm just dropping off the information you asked for." Morgan's voice was colder than an ice bath.

"Hey, Morgan. Morgan, Andrea Fletcher. Andrea, this is my agent, Morgan Gray. If you'll excuse us." He took Morgan's elbow and steered her away. "Good luck with your new job," he called over his shoulder. He escorted Morgan a distance away, and she rounded on him before he could open his mouth.

"I guess the media didn't have it all wrong." She thrust a stack of brochures at him and stormed off.

He caught up to her in a few strides. "Morgan, believe me when I tell you nothing was going on."

Her light eyes flashed in anger. "So her arms were around you because, what…she was practicing a new cheer?"

"She was trying to come on to me…again. And I told her the same thing as I did the last four times—that I wasn't interested. Didn't you see me remove her arms? Nothing else happened." She started walking again and he followed. Omar spoke to a passing teammate but waited until they reached the parking lot to continue. "Dammit, Morgan, we just spent an amazing three days together. Do you honestly believe that I would turn around and start messing around with another woman? Baby, weren't you listening to anything I said this weekend?"

"I have to go. If I have any information to share regarding your contract, I'll send you an email." She got into her car and sped off.

He cursed again, turned and went still. Malcolm stood across the lot, leaning against his motorcycle. Not in the mood to deal with anything Malcolm might have to say, he pivoted and stalked back the way he'd come. As he got closer, he could see Andrea peeking around the corner. He ignored her and kept walking until he reached the locker room.

Omar leafed through the brochures from the dance studio and slid them in the outer pocket of his duffel bag. He removed his cleats and put on his tennis shoes, then stuffed the cleats along with his sweaty clothes inside and zipped it closed.

"Problems?"

"Nothing I can't handle," he said without turning around.

Malcolm came and stood next to him. "That's my sister."

"She's a grown woman, and what goes on between us is none of your business. See you around." Without waiting for a reply, he hefted the bag onto his shoulder and strode out of the locker room.

As soon as he got home, he tried Morgan's cell, but it went straight to voice mail. Omar thought about camping out at her office until she got off, but nixed the idea when he remembered that her oldest brother worked there. He didn't need to add a confrontation with Brandon to his list today, not when he was this angry. His best bet would be to wait to get her alone. And if she thought he would settle for email communication between them, she was sadly mistaken. After this weekend, he realized his feelings for her had grown deeper, and he didn't want to go back to some casual relationship. He couldn't.

Chapter 15

Morgan paced in her kitchen, waiting for the water to heat, still angry. She didn't know who she was madder at—Omar or herself, for letting him see how upset and hurt she had been. So much for him not being like her ex. One day after confessing to missing her, he was snuggled up with someone else. The moment she spotted that tramp with her arms around him, Morgan had forgotten all about being *professional* in public.

She poured the hot water in the mug, dunked the tea bag a couple of times and waited for it to steep. She added sugar and took the cup to her bedroom. Her phone rang as she lifted it to her lips. Groaning, Morgan reached over, picked up the cordless and checked the display. When she saw Omar's name, she hesitated before replacing it. She couldn't talk to him right now and let it go to voice mail.

"Morgan, we need to talk. I don't know what it's going to take for you to believe nothing happened between me and Andrea. You can ask any guy out on the field. She came up to me only minutes before you arrived, and you saw everything—her trying to kiss me, and me telling her no. This can't work unless you trust me. You tried, convicted and sentenced me before I had a chance to take the stand. For the record, my plea is not guilty."

She set the cup on her nightstand and brought her hands up to cover her face. Why did he have to sound so sad and sincere? *I don't need this kind of drama in my life right now.* For a brief moment she thought about canceling their contract, but that would only give credence to the fact that women were too emotional to be in the business. This might be her only shot, and she refused to blow it.

Morgan's cell buzzed. *Please don't let it be him again.* She picked it up and read a text from Malcolm:

Saw you at the practice facility today. You need to talk?

She typed back:

No.

Malcolm most often let her handle her own problems and didn't interfere unless asked. She hoped this would be one of those times. She scooted against the headboard, picked up her mug and sipped, letting the warm, fragrant tea soothe her.

Hours later, she lay awake in bed, staring at the ceiling, thinking about Omar's message, his words playing over in her mind. *"You tried, convicted and sentenced me before I had a chance to take the stand...my plea is not guilty."* She tried to recall his expression when she walked up, but couldn't. Her focus had been solely on Andrea. Morgan knew that the woman was a cheerleader for the team. She also knew that there was an unspoken no-fraternization rule. Was he really as innocent as he claimed? Letting out an impatient sigh, she glanced over at the clock, flipped over and tried to shut her brain off. She had to be up at six, and that left only four hours to sleep.

It seemed as if she had just fallen asleep when her alarm went off. "Not yet," she mumbled, reaching out to shut it off. She considered going in later, but remembered today's weekly staff meeting and dragged herself out of bed. On days like this, she wished she liked coffee, because she seriously needed a pick-me-up this morning.

Morgan managed to make it to work fifteen minutes

early and had a little extra time to add some information to her weekly report. She knew her father would want an update on the test results.

"Hey, Morgan. You going down to the conference room now?"

Her head came up. "Hey, Vonnie. Yeah. I just need to print something real quick. Is Justin in today?"

"No. He's working from home. He and Brandon decided on two and a half days a week. That way Justin can work on some of his other projects." Justin had invented two safety products on his own before partnering with the family company for his latest project. He continued to work on his independent projects at home on the days he didn't come into the office.

"Smart move. Okay, I'm ready." They started down the hallway toward the conference room and were intercepted by one of the building's security guards.

"Ms. Gray? This is for you." He handed Morgan a covered travel cup and a small envelope. "Have a nice day, ladies."

"Thanks," Morgan said.

"You have the security guards bringing your order now?" Siobhan asked.

"No. I have no idea what this is." With her hands full, Morgan waited until she reached the conference room to open the envelope.

If your night was anything like mine, I know you'll need this today. I made it just how you like it with one and a half sugars.

She took a sip. Mint tea...and exactly the way she made it.

"Well, what is it?" Siobhan asked.

"Mint tea. Omar sent it." At Siobhan's confused look, she said, "I'll explain later."

"Okay. Before I forget, Mom wants to have a spa day on Saturday—just a massage and mani-pedi. Will you be up to it after the show?"

"I'll definitely need it. So count me in. What time?"

"She said ten. Then we can have lunch afterward."

"Okay."

Her father called the meeting to order, and each department gave an update.

"Morgan, where are we on the testing results for the rail?"

"John's preliminary report indicates that the rail was structurally sound, but there are a few more tests he needs to run. He anticipates having the report by the first of next week." Brandon gave her a questioning look, and she shook her head. She purposely didn't mention the glue, preferring to wait until they had conclusive determination of the substance.

"Did he indicate any possible reasons why it broke?" Uncle Thad asked.

"No. As soon as I get the results back, I'll set up a meeting so we can go over them."

Her father nodded. "Thanks, Morgan. Siobhan, I'll need you to be available for this meeting."

"No problem," Siobhan said.

The meeting lasted another twenty minutes before adjourning. Morgan stood and waved to Khalil. Although he didn't work for the company directly, he as well as Malcolm had seats on the board.

Khalil made his way over to her and kissed her cheek. "How's it going?"

"Not too bad. I saw you stuffing your face over there."

He chuckled. "I live for these meetings so I can go down

to the café and get a slice of that low-fat apple cinnamon coffee cake. Let's just say it's one of my guilty pleasures."

"Mmm-hmm. What are you drinking?"

"Vanilla chai tea. How are you and Drummond getting along?"

The real reason he came over here. "Fine. I'm confident I'll be able to get him a better deal than he has now."

"That's not what I'm talking about."

"What is it with you three guys? Do you all just sit around and plot ways to stay in my business? I'm twenty-seven, not seven. You can stand down now. And to answer your question, we're fine. Anything else?"

A smile played around the corners of Khalil's mouth. "Whatever you say, but maybe he needs to know what will happen to him if he breaks your heart."

"Don't you need to go work out or something? My heart isn't involved, and I have to go. Some of us have real work to do." She gave him a quick kiss on the cheek. "Bye." Morgan hurried off, knowing she had lied. She couldn't say for sure whether her heart was involved or not.

Wednesday afternoon, Omar slid into the booth across from Brianna and RJ and picked up his menu. The two had chosen IHOP because they hadn't decided whether to order breakfast or lunch. After a few minutes of scanning the offerings, he asked them, "Have you made a decision yet?"

"I think I'm going to have French toast," RJ said.

"I don't know," Brianna said, flipping the menu pages back and forth.

RJ sighed heavily. "We're gonna be here all day waiting for her to decide. Why do girls have to make everything so complicated?"

Omar chuckled. *I wish I had the answer to that one.* Morgan still hadn't returned his call or said anything, even after he sent her tea.

Brianna looked up from her menu. "Uncle Omar, can I order the appetizer sampler and some toast?"

"Sure, as long as you eat it."

"Oh, I'll eat it all."

After the waiter took their order, Omar took out the brochures Morgan had given him and handed them to Brianna. Omar had gotten permission from Rashad to discuss the classes. "Check these out and let me know if you see a class you like."

Her eyes lit up. *"Dance classes?"* She eagerly opened the first one and started reading.

Omar smiled and focused on his nephew. "What about you, RJ? Anything you like to do...aside from video games?"

"I want to play football."

He nodded. "Okay. But what do you want to do when football is over?"

"Maybe be an engineer like Dad."

"I think that's a great idea." Rashad had a degree in mechanical engineering, and Omar hoped his brother would heal enough to be able to return to his first love. "You should talk to him about it."

"Okay."

"Ooh, I want to do all of these classes," Brianna said. "They all look really fun."

"Well, how about we start with the one you like most."

Over lunch, Omar chatted with them about the upcoming school year and listened while they shared what they'd learned from the Black history reports they'd written. He was impressed.

"Uncle, do you have a girlfriend?"

He almost choked on his water. He stared at Brianna's smiling face. "Why?"

"I heard Mama talking, and she said your girlfriend is

pretty. Are you guys going to get married so she can be my aunt? If you are, can I be in the wedding?"

Beads of perspiration popped out on Omar's forehead. *Married? Wedding?* Okay, he liked Morgan...*a lot*, but he wasn't ready to walk down the aisle just yet. "First off, we just started dating, and second, you shouldn't eavesdrop on other people's conversations." He gestured to her plate. "You should finish your food."

RJ shook his head. "Why do you think everybody has to get married?"

"Weddings are so beautiful," she said dramatically.

RJ scrunched up his face like he'd smelled something bad and continued to eat.

Omar chuckled inwardly. At only ten, RJ still thought girls were yucky. *Keep living, little man.* He would find out that women weren't *yucky*, but absolutely amazing if you were lucky enough to find the right one. Something deep inside told him that Morgan was the right one for him. He just wished he could convince her of the same thing.

Between working and preparing for the dance show, Morgan didn't have time to dwell on her and Omar's relationship. Outside of a text she'd sent to let him know the date and time of the meeting with team management, they hadn't talked at all. As she moved around backstage at the theater, taking care of last-minute details before the show, she could admit to herself that she had missed talking to him and laughing with him. Relationships had always been a little tricky for her. Because of her bold personality, most guys either were intimidated or tried to change her. And if she had the slightest inkling something wasn't right, she would end the relationship in a heartbeat. Only this time, Morgan wasn't sure she had done the right thing.

"Ten minutes 'til showtime," Brooke called out. The kids buzzed with excitement. "Morgan, I forgot to tell you that Omar called and asked for another ticket to the show for his niece."

Morgan had totally forgotten he was coming to the show. *Just great.* "He mentioned that she was interested in taking a class. I'd better go make sure my group is ready since they're up first." If she stood there a minute longer, Brooke would have recognized something was wrong, and Morgan didn't want to hear her friend fuss.

The show went well, and while she danced, Morgan could feel Omar watching her. At the start, looking out into the audience and seeing him had thrown her off balance. It had taken all of her concentration to remember the steps and not embarrass herself on the stage. Aside from one misstep at the beginning of the song, she got through the dance without mishap. And though she knew they should talk, she needed a little more time, because what she was beginning to feel for him scared her to death. When the show ended, she changed and left quickly to avoid him. He hadn't gotten a ticket for his niece to attend the reception. She hoped that meant he had changed his mind about coming.

Omar dropped Brianna off at home and made his way over to the hotel for the reception. His niece talked nonstop all the way home. Her animated chatter made him smile, and he knew she would do well in whichever class she decided to take.

At the hotel, he handed his invitation to the young woman manning the ballroom door and entered the room. He recognized one or two prominent names in the entertainment industry. With their backing, Brooke should be well on her way to raising the money needed. Which reminded him that he needed to give her his check. He searched and found her standing in a small group. She noticed him, excused herself and came toward him.

"I'm so glad you could make it, Omar."

"You're doing some great work here."

"How did your niece like the show?"

He laughed. "She talked my ear off all the way home. She wants to take just about every class."

"Well, sign her up. We're taking a two-week break and will start up again at the beginning of August."

"I'll have my sister-in-law do that." He reached into his breast pocket, pulled out the check and handed it to her.

Brooke unfolded it and her eyes widened. "Oh. My. God. *Are you kidding me?*" She threw her arms around him. "Thank you so much." She jumped back. "Sorry. Morgan's gonna kill me if she saw that." A look of embarrassment crossed her features.

Omar smiled. "It's all good. Oh, and can you just take it as an anonymous donation?"

"Sure, but we usually list our sponsors and present them with a plaque."

"That's not necessary."

"Okay, if you insist. Thank you again." She rushed off with a huge grin.

A passing waiter offered him a glass of champagne. Omar retrieved a flute and offered a thank-you. He scanned the ballroom and saw the students and their parents all dressed up. He turned another way and froze. He didn't realize he had been holding his breath until he felt the tightness in his chest. Morgan strutted across the room wearing a long one-shoulder red dress, and with every step, he was treated to a view of her shapely legs through a slit that stopped midthigh. She'd left her hair straight, and it hung to the middle of her back. His arousal was instant. No other woman kept him hard and aching all the time. Omar tossed back the champagne and tried to remember how to breathe again. Several men stopped her, and one seemed to have trouble keeping his hands to himself. It took every bit of control he could conjure up not to go charging across the room.

"You look a little green, Drummond," an amused voice said. "Jealousy will do that to you."

He turned slightly and met Malcolm's smile. "Jealousy implies I want something that's not mine. I'm just protecting what already belongs to me. And she is mine."

"You seem pretty sure about that."

Omar's gaze strayed back to Morgan. "I am." And she would be sure about it before the night ended, because he had fallen in love with her.

Chapter 16

Morgan felt Omar's gaze following her every move. She'd spotted him the moment he walked through the door—she couldn't have missed his towering height. The eyes of every single woman in the room turned his way when he came in. In the gray suit with his locs flowing around his shoulders, he was a sight to behold. She refocused her attention on the man standing in front of her but kept stealing glances at Omar.

"You sure can dance," the man was saying.

"Thank you. Do you have a son or daughter you were thinking of enrolling?"

"Me? No. I don't have any children." He sidled closer. "I'm not married, either. Do you teach adult classes? I was hoping you could teach me some moves."

She did a mental eye roll. Was this guy for real? Teach him some moves? She smiled. "Sorry, we only teach children. If you'll excuse me, I see someone I need to speak with. Enjoy the evening. We do hope you'll support our efforts."

"Oh, yeah, yeah, sure."

Morgan left him standing there and greeted a few of the parents but never lost sight of Omar. Their eyes connected, and she could feel the pull of desire from across the room. The heat in his eyes reached out and touched her like a gentle caress.

"You know, it would be better for the two of you to pass those looks on the same side of the room, preferably while you're in proximity to each other," Brooke drawled.

Morgan frowned. "What?"

"So the rest of us don't get burned to a crisp from all the heat the both of you are generating in the room. I thought you were supposed to be seeing him secretly. If y'all don't stop with the passion eyes, everyone in a five-mile radius is going to know."

Brooke was right. Morgan needed to keep herself in check. "I'm fine. How are the donations coming?" She had set a goal of half a million dollars. The money would allow for expansion and hiring of at least two teachers, but also give them some breathing room for any repairs that might be required in the existing space.

Brooke handed Morgan a check. "We're more than half-way there with just this one donation."

Morgan read the check. "Wow."

"And he asked that I list it as anonymous. Isn't that fantastic? Girl, you picked a winner! He's fine, smart and generous." She plucked the check out of Morgan's hand. "I'm so excited."

Morgan turned his way again and found his eyes waiting. "He is all of those things." *And more*, she wanted to add. "I'm going to the bathroom. I'll be back in a minute." In reality, she only wanted to get some air and made a beeline for the hallway. One part of her wondered if he'd written such a large check just to show off, but the part of her that witnessed his passion as he spoke about the mental health center knew differently.

Morgan stared at her reflection in the bathroom mirror. She owed Omar an apology. Even though she read passion in his eyes, she also detected hurt. The drama that followed in the wake of her relationship with Jabari had made her even quicker to dismiss a relationship to protect her heart. She had told Khalil that her heart didn't factor into her and Omar's relationship, but her heart was more involved than she cared to admit.

Taking a deep breath, she smoothed down her dress

and made her way back down the long corridor toward the ballroom. Before she could get far, a hand pulled her into an empty conference room and closed the door.

"What the—"

"You're killing me, you know," Omar said in an agonized whisper, backing her against the wall.

"Omar."

"How long are you going to punish me for something I didn't do?"

"I'm not punishing you anymore. I'm sorry. I believe you when you said nothing happened."

"Thank you." Relief flooded his face, and his mouth came crashing down on hers.

The kiss was hot and demanding, making her senses spin. She felt his hand sliding up her thigh through the slit in her dress, and she shivered with the contact. He eased her panties to the side and slid in a finger. Her breath caught and she moaned, moving her hips to his lazy rhythm.

"You're the only woman I want, Morgan," he said as he transferred his kisses to her bared shoulder. "The only one, baby."

He added another finger and sped up his movements. Morgan arched against his hand, and her breath came in short gasps. He applied pressure to her clit and she convulsed.

"You're mine." Omar captured her wild cry in a deeply passionate kiss.

He withdrew, braced his hands on the wall above her head and rested his forehead against hers. "What are you doing tomorrow night?"

Still trying to recover, Morgan said, "Nothing, why?"

"My house. You, me and 'Madden.' You don't have to call. Just come." He brushed a kiss over her lips and exited the room.

Her body still trembled, and her heart pounded furiously in her chest. Fighting her feelings for him was a lost cause. At this point, she didn't want to try anymore. She leaned on a nearby table to keep from sliding to the floor. She chuckled. "Madden"? The last thing on her mind was playing a game. She wanted him to finish what he started.

Saturday morning, Morgan, Siobhan and their mother sat wearing robes and enjoying manicures and pedicures. They'd just finished a massage, and Morgan hadn't realized how much tension she'd been carrying. But now the knots and kinks were gone and she felt light as a feather.

"Morgan, I was waiting for you to introduce your young man last night," her mother said.

Siobhan leaned up and smiled.

"He's not really…" Her mother gave her a look. "We're not seeing each other publicly yet. We're waiting until his contract is done."

"I see. So how is that coming along?"

"It's going fine. The meeting is set for three weeks from now."

"Honey, you could've just told your father and me that you wanted to do this. All we want is for you to follow your heart."

"But Daddy keeps talking about me taking over the legal department sometime down the road."

"Oh, he may grumble a little bit, but he'll come around pretty quick."

Morgan doubted that but didn't say so. When Khalil decided on a career in modeling and then fitness, her father had fussed for months.

"And what's this I read about his former agent embezzling money?"

"Yeah, that's why Omar wanted a change."

"I sure hope he has a good lawyer. The man has some nerve thinking he could just steal and not get caught."

"My thoughts exactly, Mom," Siobhan chimed in. "With the amount they estimated in the papers, Roland Foster is lucky Omar didn't kick his behind."

Morgan had read the article. "I saw that Roland is denying it. And yes, Omar has a good lawyer."

"He should've asked you to do it," Siobhan said.

"Vonnie, you know I couldn't be his agent while representing him in a lawsuit against his former one."

"True, but I was thinking more about how you would wear his tail out in court."

All three women laughed and her mother said, "That's the truth."

"He did ask, though."

After finishing at the spa, they changed into their clothes and drove to a nearby restaurant for lunch. While eating, her mom went back to talking about Omar.

"You mentioned not seeing each publicly, but that doesn't mean you can't bring him to Sunday dinner. Can't get any more private than that."

Siobhan laughed. "Glad the spotlight's off me."

Morgan glared at her sister. "Mom, I'm only twenty-seven."

"I was married and had three children by then," she said.

"Shouldn't you be on Brandon more since he's the next in line? He and Khalil are already in the thirties club." They were thirty-two and thirty, respectively. Morgan thought they should be first to settle down.

"Maybe, but they aren't dating anyone seriously. You are. I'm going to tell you like I told Siobhan—if he gets out of line, don't be afraid to remind him what he'll miss if he doesn't straighten up. Nothing like a little perfume and a nice dress to make the man stand up and take notice." She wagged a finger Morgan's way. "Because you'd better believe if he takes notice, so are all the other men."

Morgan's mouth dropped and laughter escaped. "*Mom.* I can't believe you."

"What? I wasn't always this old."

Morgan and Siobhan shared a look and burst out laughing. They spent the remainder of lunch listening to their mother share her dating escapades. By the time Morgan made it home, her sides ached from laughing so hard.

After spending the bulk of the afternoon starting a time-line of events for the lawsuit, she took an hour to work out a few numbers for Omar's contract so she could discuss them after she whipped him at "Madden" again. An image of his shocked expression the last time she beat him floated through her mind and brought a smile to her face. Morgan picked up the phone to call and let him know she was on her way, but then remembered he told her just to come over, so she gathered up the papers, grabbed her purse and headed out.

"Hey, beautiful," Omar said when he opened the door. He stepped back to let her enter.

"Hey yourself, handsome. Ready for another butt-whipping?"

"Girl, you're talking smack before you get in the door. I already told you what the outcome is going to be, but I see you're choosing to ignore it. Come on in. You'll find out soon enough. I'm even prepared to feed you first to make sure you have some energy."

"Gee, thanks. Aren't you the noble one."

Omar bowed low. "At your service."

Morgan shook her head and laughed. Her laughter turned to a scream when he swooped her up and carried her through the foyer and living room to the kitchen. "I'm not really hungry. My mom, Siobhan and I spent the morning and early afternoon together, and we had a big lunch. I'll eat later, but you go ahead." She reached up and patted his cheek. "You're going to need all the help you can get."

"All right, let's go, Ms. Thang." He went through the opposite side of the kitchen to the family room and dropped down on the sofa. The game was already on pause.

She sat next to him and picked up a controller. "Same rules as last time?"

"Whatever you want, sweet baby. It doesn't matter because you're going to lose."

"In your dreams, Drummond. This time you'll be cooking my food for a week."

"We're not playing for food."

She paused. "Then what?"

"Your clothes. For every score I make, you take off an article of clothing. My choice."

"You're kidding, right?" she asked with a nervous chuckle.

He shook his head slowly. "You aren't scared, are you?"

"No way, but it won't be fair. How am I supposed to concentrate on the game if you're naked?"

"Your concentration won't be affected because all my clothes will be on."

Morgan took in his calm demeanor and felt a moment of uncertainty. Then she gave herself a pep talk. *You beat him before, so no sweat. You can do this.* "Let the game begin." When he scored in the first minute of the game, Morgan become conscious of the fact that winning might not be so easy this time.

"I think I want your top first," he said.

Because it was summer, it wouldn't take more than a few scores for them to be completely naked. She had on only four pieces of clothing—tank top, bra, shorts and panties. She'd kicked off her flip-flops as soon as she entered the house. Reaching for the hem of her top, she pulled it over her head and tossed it on the sofa next to her. Omar leaned over and trailed his tongue over the tops of her breasts visible above the bra.

"Your turn," he murmured, taking her mouth in an intoxicating kiss.

Clearing her mind from the sensual fog he'd placed her in, Morgan took her turn. She was one yard from scoring when Omar caused her man to fumble. He picked up the ball and returned it for a touchdown. Morgan stared at the TV in disbelief.

"I'm not sure what I want to see more, your beautiful breasts or your luscious hips in the pair of sexy panties I know you're wearing." He scooted closer, then ran his hand up her torso and around her back and unhooked her bra. "They were calling me." He cupped one breast in each hand and massaged and kneaded them.

Omar used his thumbs to tease the hardened buds, and her breath caught. When he lowered his head and replaced his thumbs with his tongue, she moaned and fell back against the sofa. He captured her nipples between his teeth and tugged gently. "Baby," she said, "we're supposed to be…ooh…playing…ooh…"

"Sorry." He helped her to an upright position.

Morgan didn't know how she could concentrate on playing with her body in such turmoil. By halftime she was down to her panties and had yet to claim one piece of his clothing.

"I know how we can spend halftime." Omar lifted her to straddle his lap, and the wandering caresses began again. "I can't stop touching you."

She took hold of his locs and fastened her mouth on his in a deep, scorching kiss. She captured his tongue and sucked hard, eliciting a hoarse groan from him. It was her turn to groan when his hands slipped beneath her panties to grip her buttocks and grind her against his erection. Morgan's hands went to the waistband of his shorts, but he removed her hands.

"Game's not over yet, sweetheart," he panted and sat her back on the sofa. "You first."

She finally scored a touchdown at the beginning of the fourth quarter and decided to get some sweet revenge. "I'll take those shorts."

He stood and pushed the shorts down and off, leaving him clad in a T-shirt and a pair of black boxer briefs. "You have only two minutes to score fourteen points."

"Mmm-hmm." She ran her hand over the rock-solid ridge of his shaft through the briefs. His head fell back, and a low moan erupted from his throat. She knelt in front of him and replaced her hand with her tongue, and Omar's breath became uneven. "I do believe it's your turn."

Still breathing harshly, he picked up the controller, promptly marched downfield and scored a touchdown. His mouth curved in a wicked grin.

Morgan couldn't believe she'd lost the game, and by twenty-one points. She stood to remove her last piece of clothing, and he shook his head.

"Nah, baby, this honor belongs to me."

He slowly stripped her panties away, using the fabric and his fingers to tantalize and excite her until she was wet. He positioned her on the edge of the sofa and lifted her legs onto his shoulders, kissing his way up to her left inner thigh, then the right. At the first swipe of his hot tongue on her center, Morgan's hips flew off the couch. She gripped the edge to hold on as he plunged his tongue deep inside her. She was already so aroused that it didn't take long for the orgasm to slam into her.

Omar shed the rest of his clothes, grabbed his shorts, searched the pockets and extracted condoms. He tore one off, tossed the others aside and quickly sheathed himself. Coming back to where Morgan still lay trembling, he entered her fully in one deep thrust.

She arched up and cried out. He set a driving motion,

and she matched his fluid movements. He whispered erotic endearments that pushed her closer and closer to the edge until she screamed out his name. He pulled out, turned her around and surged back in. She screamed again.

"I love how your body fits mine," he said without slowing.

She threw her hips back at him. "So do I," she murmured. He grasped her hips and thrust harder and faster. *"Omar!"* Morgan was hit by an orgasm so strong it snatched her breath and nearly made her pass out.

Omar went rigid against her, then bucked and shuddered as he climaxed right behind her, yelling her name loud enough to be heard throughout the entire neighborhood. He collapsed over her back with a harsh groan of satisfaction. Slowly he drew them down to the floor.

She rested her head on his heaving chest and could hear his rapidly beating heart. "If this is what happens when I lose, I may be inclined to lose more often," she said tiredly.

His low chuckle rumbled against her ear. "Yeah, I hear you."

Silence rose between them, and Morgan could barely keep her eyes open.

"I don't think I have the energy to cook. We're going to have to order in."

"Fine by me, but no rush. I don't think I can move right now."

"That makes two of us."

As they lay there, Morgan knew she would never see "Madden" the same again. She also accepted the fact that she was in love with Omar. For the time being, she decided it might be best to keep that information to herself. If he knew how she felt, he would, without a doubt, want to go public. And that was something she couldn't do... at least not yet.

Chapter 17

Monday morning, Omar stood on the deck off his bedroom, reminiscing about his weekend with Morgan. He felt himself smile. The surprise on her face when she lost the game was priceless—although in his mind, they both had come out winners. The heated images flooded his mind and sent a jolt of desire straight to his groin. They'd had a second round after ordering and eating Chinese, and he convinced her to spend the night. Just like the previous weekend, waking up next to her seemed right, and he wouldn't have minded starting his morning with her every day. He had planned to tell her he loved her but never found the right time. He didn't want to say it during sex because he didn't want her to think it was the lust talking. But then, he'd never said those words to a woman before and realized that might be another reason he had held back.

Turning, he went back inside and left for his run. Omar started with an easy pace then picked up speed until he was at a full sprint. His thoughts went to the article he had seen in the paper about his pending lawsuit against Roland. He couldn't believe the comments Roland had made. How did he think Omar wouldn't notice, and why deny it when there was solid proof? Jaedon had called Omar and asked him to meet later this morning. He was curious about what the attorney had found out.

He changed direction and took the hill on the next block. The familiar burn started in his chest and legs, but he welcomed it. Once he returned home, he spent the next hour in his home gym, then showered.

Omar walked through the doors of Dupree and Montgomery ten minutes before his scheduled appointment time. While waiting, he took the opportunity to send Morgan a text asking if they could get together that evening or the next. He planned to tell her he loved her and convince her to go public with their relationship. He was tired of hiding and wanted to introduce her to his parents.

"Mr. Drummond, Mr. Dupree will see you now."

He thanked the assistant, stood and followed her to Jaedon's office.

"Thanks, Yvonne," Jaedon said as she exited. He shook Omar's hand. "Have a seat."

"You said you have some information."

Jaedon nodded. "I asked a friend of mine to join us. He's the private investigator I mentioned. It looks like Roland has been busy. There are at least two other players he's embezzled from."

Omar sighed. "I saw that article. He's denying everything."

"And insinuating you're doing it as a publicity stunt."

His anger rose. "How long before this mess gets settled?"

"Depends on—" A soft knock sounded and the door opened.

"Sorry to interrupt," the assistant said, "but you asked me to escort Mr. Wright in when he arrived."

"No problem. Come on in, Zo. Omar Drummond, this is Alonzo Wright. Zo—"

"This man needs no introduction," Alonzo said, extending his hand. "End Zone Drummond. Good to meet you, man."

"Same here," Omar said, rising to shake the proffered hand.

They all sat and Jaedon continued. "As I was saying, the length of time it could take depends on how long Mr. Foster tries to drag things out. I have a meeting with his attorney tomorrow, and we'll see how it goes. My hope is that the man will realize he doesn't have a leg to stand on and end this fiasco. I'm already working to get a warrant for his arrest. Zo, did you find out anything else on Omar's endorsements?"

"Nothing aside from the three we already knew about. It looks like he was trying to broker another deal."

Omar nodded. "He'd called me about it, but it was the day I fired him, so he can't negotiate anything on my behalf. I contacted the representative from Apple to let them know my new agent would be in touch."

"I did observe him meeting with a woman at a coffee shop a few times," Alonzo said.

"Must be his assistant, Carolyn."

"Assistant?" Alonzo stroked his chin. "Maybe, but the woman always seems to be nervous coming and going."

Omar shrugged. "I can't help you. Do you know what she looks like?" Alonzo described a woman who could have been Carolyn. He'd only seen her twice and couldn't be sure.

"I plan to keep them under surveillance a little longer to see what he's up to, and I'll get a couple of pictures to send Jaedon so you can take a look."

"Sounds good. I appreciate it."

"No problem. Looking forward to seeing you on the field this season." Alonzo stood. "I'll be in touch, Jae." And then he was gone.

Omar and Jaedon talked a few more minutes before the meeting ended. On the drive home, Omar thought about the conversation and what Alonzo revealed, and got angry all over again. Why would Roland be meeting with his assistant at a coffee shop instead his office? Shaking off the negative vibes, he decided to drive across town to the restaurant. He'd promised his mother he would stop by.

His mother took one look at him when he came through

the door and declared, "Praise God! The prodigal son has returned." That garnered a few chuckles and curious stares from the diners.

He walked behind the bar and hugged and kissed her. "Seriously, Mom. It's only been about three weeks."

She eyed him. "More like a month. It's not like you live in another state."

Omar gave her a sheepish grin. "I know."

"And you can't use football as an excuse."

He kissed her again. "I'm sorry. You know I love you."

"Mmm-hmm, stop trying to butter me up."

"What?" he asked innocently. "I do love you."

She popped him on the arm. "Go sit down, boy. You want something to eat?"

"Just some chicken soup."

"All right. I'll have Joanne bring it out to you."

The lunch crowd had come and gone, so more than half of the tables sat empty. Omar slid into a booth near the back, away from the other diners. His cell buzzed. He pulled it out and read the text from Morgan.

Might be tough with my workload, but maybe we can meet for a few minutes tomorrow night. What are you doing?

At the family restaurant. Mom's been on my case since I haven't visited in a few weeks.

He glanced up at Joanne's approach.

"Hey, Omar. Here's your soup. Can I get you anything else?"

"Thanks, Joanne. May I have a glass of water?"

"Sure. Be right back."

The phone buzzed again.

There had better not be anything resembling BBQ ribs on your plate.

Omar chuckled and replied,

Just soup, baby. I promise to hold off on the ribs until I bring you.

OK. Gotta run.

"What are you back here smiling about?" his mother asked, placing a glass of water on the table and sitting across from him.

"Just talking to a friend."

"It's good to see you, Omar. How've you been?" his father asked, joining them.

"Hey, Dad." He started to rise.

His father shook his head. "Don't get up."

"I'm good," Omar said. "Just making a few transitions."

"And why is it that I have to read in the paper about this mess with Roland and that you have a new agent?"

"That's part of the reason I haven't been around."

"Are you going to be able to get your money back?" his father asked.

"I hope so."

His mother smiled. "Your father showed me the picture of your new agent. She's beautiful, but how much does she really know about football?"

Memories of that "Madden" game they'd played flashed in his head, along with the resulting sensations. "Ah, she knows a lot," he answered, bringing the spoon to his mouth.

"I don't know how wise it is to take on someone who's new to the business at this stage of your career."

Omar replaced the spoon in the bowl. "Dad, Morgan

Gray is an attorney. She works for her family's company, Gray Home Safety. Her brother is a teammate, and he says she knows the game well." The fact that she was the first person ever to beat him at the video game's highest level left him no doubts that she knew football.

His mother angled her head thoughtfully. "I see. And when will we get to meet this young lady?"

He shrugged. "Not sure." That their relationship was supposed to be secret didn't lend itself to him bringing her to the restaurant, where everyone knew him and would be sure to have questions. Pictures would be all over social media within seconds of their arrival.

"I'm anxious to meet the woman who has captured my son's heart."

Omar didn't know whose face registered more shock, his or his father's.

"You're dating your agent?" his father asked incredulously.

He released a deep sigh and nodded. "Yes, but—"

"But, what? You're either dating her or not."

"We've agreed to keep it under wraps until the new contract is done. This is her first shot at the business, and I don't want to jeopardize that." But he also didn't know how much longer he would be able to hold out.

His mother reached for his hand. "She sounds like a wonderful person, and I can't wait to meet her."

"She is." He found himself utterly captivated by every facet of her personality.

"As long as she makes you happy, sweetheart, don't worry about anything else. Let's go, Bobby, so Omar can finish his food." They scooted out of the booth, and she placed a motherly kiss on his brow.

His father patted his shoulder. "Good luck, son. I hope it works out."

"Thanks, Dad." He hoped it did, too. He wasn't sure what he'd do if things fell apart.

Against her better judgment, Morgan agreed to meet Omar Tuesday downstairs at the café located on the first floor of the office building. But if they both could keep a business-like appearance, everything should be fine. John's test results on the rail had come back and Mr. Metzler indicated his report would be sent today, so she would be spending her time getting ready for the meeting with Mr. Porter later in the week. Consequently she wouldn't be available tonight, as she'd previously thought. Morgan had purposely chosen a later time to ensure they'd miss the lunch crowd. When she spotted him and their eyes connected, everything she felt rose to the surface, and she had a hard time not rushing across the room and kissing him.

"Hey." Omar lowered himself into a chair.

"Hey. You said you needed to tell me something and it couldn't wait." He seemed to be weighing his words before speaking, and the hairs on the back of her neck stood up.

Omar nodded. "I didn't want to do this in a public place, but I need to tell you something."

"What is it? Did something happen?" He grasped her hands. Mindful of where they were, Morgan tried to pull back, but he tightened his hold.

"Baby, I don't want to hide anymore."

"Omar, we talked about this," she said in hushed tones.

"I know we did, and I was okay with it at first."

"It's only a couple more weeks. Just a little while longer," she pleaded.

"I can't." He leaned forward and locked his gaze on hers. "I love you, Morgan, and I want to tell the world."

Her pulse skipped. "Omar... I... I don't know what to say. Are you sure? I mean, we haven't been together long." *"I love you, too," might work*, her inner voice chimed.

Omar smiled. "I realize that, but it doesn't change what's in here." He pointed to his heart.

Morgan closed her eyes. *Tell him!* "I…"

"I'm in this for the long haul, so I can wait until you—"

"I already do," she whispered. He stared at her with such tenderness she thought her heart would explode. "But I'm not ready for everyone to know."

"Morgan."

"I need a few days to think about it, okay. Please?"

He gave her hands a gentle squeeze and released them. "Okay. When is your meeting about the lawsuit?"

"Friday."

"Maybe we can talk it over Friday evening before training camp starts on Saturday."

"Yes." Their meeting with the Cobras was scheduled for the middle of next week, and she had been thinking they would casually start being seen together a week or so afterward. But his confession had completely thrown her for a loop.

"I'll see you later, sweetheart."

Morgan nodded and watched him stride out. Blowing out a long breath, she went back up to her office.

"I left your messages on your desk," Evelyn said as Morgan passed.

"Thank you." She closed the door, dropped down in her chair and rubbed her temples. She couldn't be happier that he loved her, but she still worried how it would affect her goals. Her gaze strayed to the stack of messages. She rifled through them and, seeing that none were urgent, laid them aside. She picked up the pad holding her notes for Omar's contract. She had compared salaries and stats of all the league's tight ends and knew she should be able to get him somewhere near, if not at the top of, the salary cap, along with more guaranteed money. Excitement raced through her veins. If this went well, it would show other players that she could, indeed, hang with the big boys.

Morgan's computer chimed an incoming email, and she quickly clicked on the message from Mr. Metzler, happy to see the promised report attached. She read over the results. "I don't believe it," she mumbled. She snatched up the receiver and called Brandon.

"Brandon Gray."

"Hey, big brother. Just got Mr. Metzler's report. The findings support the ones in John's report."

"Then, this whole ordeal will be over soon."

"Keep your fingers crossed. Talk to you later."

Morgan placed the papers she had been working on in their folder, tossed it on the corner of her desk and pulled the file containing the lawsuit documents. She printed the report and worked on the timeline. She frowned. Something didn't add up. Digging through the mess of paperwork, she located the delivery tracking receipt. "That can't be right, unless…" She picked up the emergency room report and smiled. "Bingo."

Friday afternoon, Morgan made sure she had all the packets of information, then headed down to the conference room where her father, sister, brother and uncle were all waiting. She greeted everyone and took a seat. Minutes later, her father's assistant, Mrs. Avery, escorted in Mr. Porter. Morgan successfully concealed her surprise at seeing his clients, the Sandersons, enter behind him. Mrs. Sanderson was in a wheelchair being pushed by her husband.

"Thank you for coming," Morgan said, gesturing the trio to the table.

"My clients insisted on being present," Mr. Porter said.

After introductions were made, Morgan asked, "Would either of you like some coffee or tea before we get started?"

They all declined. "I have the reports from both our office and from Mr. Metzler." She passed out the copies. "You will see that both reports conclude the structural integrity of the rail is intact."

"That doesn't matter," Mr. Porter interrupted. "It still came away from the wall, and my client was injured as a result."

Morgan smiled. "We're very sorry about Mrs. Sanderson's accident. To make things easier, if you turn to page seven, I took the liberty of recreating a timeline of events." She waited. "According to the tracking receipt in your packet, the rails were delivered on a Thursday at 1:27 in the afternoon. Estimated installation time can be anywhere from two to four hours, depending on a person's expertise. I call your attention to the highlighted lines. Those are the dates and times the ambulance arrived and when Mrs. Sanderson was admitted to emergency."

"All of this means nothing," Mr. Porter said impatiently.

Morgan turned her attention to Mr. Sanderson and asked gently, "Mr. Sanderson, were there instructions included in the kit?"

"Yes."

She felt really bad about what she had to do, but slid the instructions to the man. "Can you please tell me what the circled section says?"

He picked up the paper and his eyes widened. Mr. Sanderson glanced up at Morgan and lowered his head.

Seemingly confused, Mr. Porter looked from Mr. Sanderson to Morgan. "What is going on here?"

Morgan took the liberty of passing the attorney another copy of the instructions. "The circled portion clearly states in a large, bold and italic font to wait twenty-four hours after installation before using to allow the included glue to adhere to the surface. Less than ten hours passed between delivery of the rails and Mrs. Sanderson's injury. In addition, your client did *not* use our glue. Please turn to page eight. Tests conducted on the sticky substance on the ends of the rails seen in the photo indicate that Mr. Sanderson used an over-the-counter superglue. These results show that, while we sympathize with your clients, Gray Home Safety is not liable for Mrs. Sanderson's injuries."

The couple looked crushed, and Morgan's heart went out to them. However, she was happy to prove her family's company hadn't been at fault. With nothing else left to say, Mr. Porter led his clients out. She breathed a sigh of relief. Her family's praise filled her with a sense of pride, and her father asked to talk to her alone.

"What is it, Dad?"

"I can't tell you how proud I am of you, sweetheart. Your tenacity saved us millions of dollars, not to mention our reputation."

Morgan knew where he was headed.

"Honey, I really wish you would reconsider this whole agent thing."

"Dad, this is what I want to do, and I may not get another shot. I have to take this chance. Otherwise, I'll always wonder *what if?*"

He sighed deeply and nodded. "And if it doesn't work out?"

"Then you'll be stuck with me here," she said with a wry chuckle. They shared a smile.

"I love you, baby girl." He engulfed her in a warm hug.

"I love you, too, Daddy."

He placed a kiss on her forehead. "Give 'em hell." He winked and left her standing there.

With the late hour, Morgan packed up and went home. Having her family's blessings, especially her parents', meant a lot, and Morgan felt as if a huge weight had been lifted off her shoulders. And now that the lawsuit had been cleared up, she could focus solely on the contract over the weekend. She was also anxious to see Omar, but he'd called to let her know that he might not make it over because his sister-in-law had been involved in a traffic accident. And with the start of training camp tomorrow, she resigned herself with having to wait to tell him her decision. She was ready to risk it all for them.

Chapter 18

Monday morning, Omar eased down in his seat and waited for the tight ends meeting to begin. Luckily, the Cobras team management opted not to travel for camp, which afforded a player the ability to stay in the comfort of his own home instead of living in a hotel or dorm for weeks. After arriving at the practice facility at seven, he'd completed almost an hour of conditioning and strength training and had breakfast. But his thoughts were never far from Morgan.

He couldn't go to her on Friday because Serena had been involved in a car accident, and he'd gone over to stay with Brianna and RJ while Rashad accompanied her to the hospital. Thankfully, aside from some soreness, she was fine. But by the time they made it home, it was too late to visit Morgan. Then with the start of training camp Saturday, he hadn't had a free moment. Omar planned to call her tonight when he got back home, but most likely he wouldn't be able to see her until Wednesday at the meeting. As much as he missed her, it was going to take a herculean effort for him not to grab her up and kiss her like he wanted. He was curious as to how she would do with the team's owner, Lawler and the general manager, Green, especially since she would be shooting for the top of the cap and more money up front. Both men could be somewhat brusque. Then again, she had handled Roland with no problems. That coupled with the knowledge that they could be open with their relationship in a few days put a smile on his face.

"What's got you in a good mood so early in the morning, Drummond?"

Omar glanced up at his teammate. "What's up, Todd? It's a good day."

Todd Elliot dropped into a seat, leaving one chair between them. "Must be. Heard you had a new agent, and she's fine as hell."

"I hired her for her knowledge of the game, not for her looks." He curbed the urge to say what he really wanted, but added, "Oh, and if I were you, I'd be careful what you say about her. I don't think her brother would take too kindly to it."

Todd slanted him a glance. "Who's her brother?"

"Malcolm Gray." Todd didn't get a chance to reply because the tight ends coach entered with one other player, but judging by the man's expression, Omar had gotten his point across. When the meeting ended, it was time to hit the practice field.

By the end of the day with the evening walk-through, he was more than ready to grab a bite to eat and go home. As he was leaving, one of his teammates called out to him.

"Wait up, Drummond."

He shifted his duffel to the other shoulder and waited.

"Hey, man. I heard about what your agent is going for in your contract. I hope she can pull it off."

"What are you talking about?"

"You haven't seen it?" He dug out his cell and brought up an article.

Omar read it, and his heart nearly stopped. He handed the phone back. "Thanks. I'll see you later."

"Is she looking to increase her roster?"

"I don't know," he said without turning around. And he didn't care. Once again, a woman only looking to use him for her fifteen minutes of fame had fooled him. This time it hurt more than he could have ever imagined.

* * *

Tuesday evening, Morgan tried to call Omar again. He hadn't responded to her text earlier, and she knew the team was done for the day. She had a new thought with respect to his contract she wanted to talk to him about before the meeting tomorrow. There was no practice, and she hoped they could have some time to talk afterward. The call went to voice mail.

"Hey, Omar. Give me a call as soon as you can. I'd like to go in a different direction than what we discussed. It would give you a little more money if we can pull it off, but I want to run it by you first. If we don't get a chance to talk tonight, we can talk briefly before the meeting. I'll be there at nine forty-five."

She started to worry when he didn't return her call, but remembered that Malcolm often stayed to himself during camp, especially the first couple of weeks.

After a fitful night, Morgan dressed in a conservative gray skirt suit and black pumps, inspected herself once more and left. She saw Omar drive into the lot as she stepped out of her car. She waited for him to park and met him halfway. She smiled. "Good morning. Did you get my message?"

Omar drilled her with an angry stare. "Let's just cut the bull and get this over with."

Morgan was taken aback by his tone. "I don't understand."

"The next time you want to go all out for the media, leave me out of it."

Dread uncoiled in her belly. "What the hell are you talking about? What media?"

"Don't stand here and pretend you don't know what I'm talking about," he gritted out.

"I don't," she snapped.

"So, the media got that quote by themselves." He spared her one last glare and stalked off.

Morgan was so outdone, she didn't know what to do. She fished her cell out of her purse and searched in sports news. What she found weakened her knees. She hadn't told anyone about her plans. How did the media get wind of those figures? They were the ones she initially talked to Omar about, but not the new ones. She caught up to him inside.

"I didn't do this, Omar."

He ignored her and kept walking.

"You can't possibly believe I would do something like this," she whispered harshly. "And if you had responded to my calls and messages over the past two days, you'd know that." The office door opened and team's owner, Mr. Lawler, waved them in. Morgan schooled her features and placed a smile on her face. "Good morning, Mr. Lawler. Morgan Gray." She turned to the general manager and nodded a greeting. "Mr. Green."

"Ms. Gray, it's a pleasure. Good to see you, Omar. Please have a seat."

Omar shook hands with the men and sat. "Same here."

Morgan took a couple of calming breaths to rein in her temper. She was sorely tempted to walk out and let Omar deal with it on his own, but that would just ruin everything she had worked to accomplish. Never being one to cower, she decided to meet the challenge head-on. "It has just come to my attention that there have been statements in the media supposedly made by me regarding these negotiations. I assure you I did not release any information, but I *will* find out who did." She skewered Omar with a look.

"We appreciate your candidness, Ms. Gray," the owner said.

"Thank you."

Mr. Green nodded. "I don't have to tell you how integral Omar is to our team." He proceeded to provide a long list of Omar's accomplishments, detailing how well he fit with the team currently and within the future vision. He gave high praise for the way Omar had filled in last season with the injury of one of their receivers.

Morgan waited until he finished. "I agree that Omar has filled a critical role in the Cobras organization. And my client is prepared to continue bringing the same dedication this season in that role." She smiled inwardly when she saw the moment they understood.

Mr. Green's brow lifted. "Are you suggesting we move Omar to the wide receiver position?"

"You said it yourself—he's a valuable asset. We all know that Colin won't be returning for the first half of the season, at best. It's a known fact that without him, you're weak on the left side. I know it and so do the other thirty-one teams. Until my client stepped in last season, you were O-and-four."

"Granted, we're grateful for the way he's played for us, but changing positions is just not done."

"Not according to the three other teams who have been ringing my phone." Out of the corner of her eye, she saw surprise cross Omar's face. "Or the ten games he played as your wide receiver last season. And at a great bargain to the team, I might add."

"I'm not sure we can do this."

"Omar's numbers were second only to Marcus Dupree's…in the league. He went over and above, and is the reason you made it to the playoffs. This is his home, and he's committed to winning. He knows the playbook. The time it would take for you to develop another player could cost you a trip to the playoffs. Do you want to risk missing the opportunity to bring a Super Bowl win to your fans?" Morgan remained calm on the outside, but on the inside her heart raced and butterflies danced in her belly.

She could see the wheels turning in both men's heads and almost feel their surrender. When it came, she wanted to shout for joy.

"We're willing to settle for sixty million over the next four years, which is a bargain compared to the eighty million he's worth, plus a signing bonus, performance incentives and more guaranteed money."

After several more minutes of discussion, the meeting ended with handshakes. As she and Omar pushed through the doors leading to the parking lot, Morgan thought she might burst from excitement. The only thing marring this perfect moment was the tension and anger between her and Omar. Once they were near her car, she stopped and rounded on him.

"Do you actually believe I would risk your career and mine by being foolish enough to brag to the media about a potential contract? Even if I were that arrogant, I wouldn't do it, because I love you." She chuckled bitterly. "Funny, you said that I had to trust you in order for this to work. Too bad that only goes one way. I guess I'm not the only one acting as judge, jury and executioner. Congratulations. You get to end your career at home and as a wide receiver. I'll mail you the forms so you can exercise the exit clause. Then you can be free to find a more trustworthy agent." Not bothering to wait for his response, she spun on her heel, covered the short distance to her car, got in and drove off without a backward glance. Only when she hit the freeway did she acknowledge the pain surrounding her heart and let the tears fall.

Morgan moved through the office like a ghost for the remainder of the week, closing out the case and working with Siobhan on press releases. She'd also had to field questions from the media regarding her entrance into the world of sports management. Through it all, she kept a smile on her face.

At the family dinner Sunday afternoon, Morgan picked at her food. Animated conversation flowed around her, but she couldn't muster up the energy to contribute. Her family had decided to have an additional get-together to celebrate her successes at the company and in negotiating her first contract. And since there was no football practice, Malcolm joined them. He watched her like a hawk and had been reluctant to leave her side for one moment, so much so that he had helped with the cooking.

"Morgan, I heard that you signed on another player," her father said. "How many is that now?"

"Two." Less than three days after news broke about the deal she had brokered for Omar, two of his teammates had called her—the star quarterback, whose current agent would be retiring from the business due to illness, and a defensive end in his second year who would be a force to be reckoned with in coming years.

"Is everything okay, sweetheart?" her mother asked, studying Morgan critically.

"I'm good, Mom. Just coming off an adrenaline high. I think I might take a few days off next week and get out of Dodge for a bit." Omar's cabin flashed through her mind, along with everything they had done over their weekend. The sadness that had been her constant companion since Wednesday threatened to overwhelm her once more, but she forced it back. It was time to move on. *If it's time to move on, why haven't you mailed those papers?* She signed the papers dissolving her and Omar's partnership, but had not sent them to him as yet. Because part of her knew that sending those papers would represent the end of their relationship.

Omar should have been celebrating…in more ways than one. He couldn't get over how Morgan turned Green's words on him and had the man believing he'd just gotten

away with the deal of the century. Because of her, he would
be back to his preferred position, and at an average yearly
salary that damn near doubled his current one.

But the general manager wasn't the only person whose
words had come back to haunt him. Omar kept seeing the
hurt in her eyes when she had thrown his back in his face.
Had he judged her unfairly? And if he was wrong, how
did the media get a direct quote from her? He pondered
the question for the entire ride home and still didn't have
an answer by the time he arrived. He knew his family
was awaiting news about the contract, but in his present
mood, he didn't feel like talking and sent a group text. All
he wanted was to go back to three days ago when everything in his life had been perfect.

Over the next three practice days, Omar tried to bury
his emotions in order to get through the daily grind. Not
an easy feat when player after player, after offering congratulations, made mention of Morgan. It only served to
make him miss her more. He'd even had a couple of inqui-
ries whether she would be willing to take on new clients.
He could only answer, "You'll have to ask her."

The more he thought on it, the more he realized that he
might have made a mistake. None of what he read came
up in the meeting. He had finally listened to the message
she had left regarding a new direction, and it only con-
jured up more questions. He'd picked up the phone several times but didn't know what to say and hung up before
the call completed. Despite the distance between them,
the love he felt for her still burned bright. His nights were
filled with memories of her smile, the kisses they shared
and the most erotic game of "Madden" he'd ever played.
And each morning, he woke up hard and reaching for her.

After practice ended for the day on Saturday, Omar
showered and made his way to the lot. His steps slowed
upon seeing Malcolm leaning against Omar's truck. "Not

today," he muttered. Actually, he was surprised it had taken this long for Malcolm to approach him. "Something on your mind, Gray?"

"My sister didn't do what you accused her of. You're my teammate and a friend, but my brothers and I promised ourselves that the next guy to break our sister's heart would get his ripped out. So far, she's managed to save your sorry ass, but don't count on it lasting. If she sheds one more tear, all bets are off." Malcolm straightened from his position and strode off.

Omar's heart sped up, but not from fear. Morgan didn't strike him as a woman who cried, so for her to do so meant something. Pain ripped through his chest. He wanted to hold her in his arms and kiss away the hurt he had caused. He had to find a way to make things right and would do whatever it took to accomplish the task. Even begging.

Chapter 19

Wednesday afternoon, Morgan started to her bedroom with a cup of tea to pick up where she left off in the mystery thriller she was reading. Being off work this week and unplugging from social media had done wonders for her mind. Halfway there the doorbell rang. Her siblings had been taking turns dropping by to check on her, despite her many protests that she was fine. Since it was the middle of the day, she placed her bet on Khalil. Being owner of the fitness center meant no set hours. She changed direction and went to answer the door. Morgan almost dropped her cup when she saw Omar standing there. She stared into the handsome face that wouldn't leave her memory. He wore a sleeveless tank and shorts, showing off the sculpted muscles of his arms. With his hair flowing loose around his shoulders, the man looked good enough to eat. It took everything within her to stand there and not drag him inside for another round of their special version of "Madden."

Omar's gaze roamed over her from head to toe and back up again. They stared at each other for what seemed like forever. Finally he said, "Hey."

"What are you doing here?"

"May I come in? Please," he added when she didn't move.

She stepped back for him to enter. He moved past her and continued to her living room. Groaning inwardly, she closed the door and followed. She sat as far away from him as she could and didn't say one word.

"I brought these back." He held up an envelope.

She recognized it as the one she had finally sent. "You could've saved yourself some gas and mailed them."

"I didn't sign them."

"Why not? I thought that's what you wanted."

"I never said I wanted to opt out. You did."

Morgan set her cup on the table and massaged her temples. There was no way she could continue to represent him under these circumstances. "Omar, I can't—"

"I don't want to opt out on us, either."

Her head snapped up. "What are you talking about?"

"I love you, Morgan, and I was wrong. I'm sorry I accused you of going to the media behind my back."

As much as she wanted to hear those words, it was too late. "How about I accept your apology and we move on."

Omar raked a hand down his face. "Move on? I *can't* move on, not without you, baby," he said emotionally.

Fighting to remain impassive, she stood and walked to the door. "You don't have a choice."

He crossed the room and turned her face toward his. "I can't give you up, sweetheart. You mean too much to me. I'll go, but we're not over...not by a long shot." He brushed his lips across hers and then left.

Morgan rested her forehead against the door, still feeling the effects of the soft kiss. She wanted to give in so bad, to feel his arms around her again. Why did this have to hurt so much?

She had just gotten settled with her book when the doorbell rang again. *Please don't let it be him.* Sliding off the bed, she went out front and, this time, peered through the peephole. Sighing in relief, she opened the door. "Hey, Vonnie."

"You look a mess," Siobhan said, brushing past Morgan. "It's a good thing I stopped by." She dropped down on the sofa. "You must have talked to Omar."

"How do you know that?"

"Your face says it all. I remember having the same look when things went south with Justin and me. What happened?"

"He just left a little while ago. He didn't sign the papers opting out of his contract, and he said he's not giving up on us."

"And how do you feel about that?"

"I don't know. One side of me says great. The other side is afraid something like this could happen again."

"Does he still think you blabbed to the media?"

"No, and he apologized."

Siobhan patted the space next to her, and Morgan slid onto the sofa. Siobhan grasped her hand. "Well, it sounds like he's owned up to his mistake. How do you feel about Omar?"

"I love him."

"And how does he feel?"

"He says he loves me."

"Honey, understand that relationships are not always cut-and-dried. And lasting ones will require some sacrifice on both your parts. He's made his position clear. If you love him, the only thing left for you to decide is whether you'll be happy without him in your life."

Morgan laid her head on her sister's shoulder. "How did you know that Justin was the right one?"

"I didn't, but my heart did. And so will yours."

She hoped it would tell her something soon, because the only thing she knew was that her heart hurt.

Omar dropped down heavily on his bed and removed his shoes. It had been four days since he walked out of Morgan's house, and his concentration during practice was at an all-time low. She had told him he had no choice but to move on, but his heart had decided otherwise. He fished his cell out of his pocket and turned it on. Almost immediately, a series of chimes sounded, indicating several missed messages. He had two emails and a text from Jaedon asking Omar to call as soon as possible. He sighed wearily and prayed there was some good news about his case against Roland. He decided to read the emails before calling. The first one detailed the second meeting with Roland's attorney and gave Omar hope that this nightmare wouldn't last much longer. Since the agent's arrest a week ago, the media had been hounding Omar between practices. He just offered a standard "no comment" and kept it moving.

The second email was one forwarded from Alonzo. He was able to get a picture of the woman who had been meeting with Roland. He clicked on the attachment and felt his eyes widen. Omar quickly dialed Jaedon's cell.

"Hey, Omar," Jaedon said. "I'm glad you called."

"I just got home from practice and saw your messages. Roland is out on bail?"

"Yes."

"Probably using money that doesn't belong to him."

"That's a possibility, but I've asked the judge to freeze all his assets until we can sort it out. Did you get a chance to look at the picture Zo took?"

"Yeah."

"Is it his secretary?"

"No."

"No? Do you recognize her?"

"I do." He filled Jaedon in on what he knew and the last time he had seen her. *The article.* "I have to go. I'll call you back in a little while. There's someone I need to talk to."

"Is everything okay?"

"No. But, I'm hoping I can fix some of it. I'll fill you in when I call you."

Omar disconnected, put his shoes on and left. Thirty

minutes later, he pulled up in a driveway, hopped out and went to ring the doorbell. The door swung open.

"Drummond? What are you doing here?"

"I need to talk to you."

Malcolm eyed him briefly. "Come in."

He followed Malcolm through the foyer, living room and kitchen to the family room.

"You want something to drink?"

"No, thanks."

"Something happen with my sister?"

He brought up the picture by way of answer. "Recognize her?"

"Yes, but why is she with Roland?"

"I think they may be responsible for that bogus story about my contract." It would have been easy for Roland to plant that false story with all his media contacts.

Malcolm muttered a curse. "What are you planning to do?"

"Let Jaedon handle it. If he can prove they were in it together, it'll clear Morgan's name." The article insinuated that Morgan had revealed the information as a way to boost her credibility.

"Why do you care?"

"I messed up, but I love your sister. If I can get her back, she'll never shed another tear." They engaged in a stare-down for several tense moments before Malcolm nodded. "What about Morgan? She needs to know."

"Since there's no practice tomorrow, I'll go by the office. My brother Brandon and I will handle it."

"Can you let me know how she is afterward?"

"Yeah."

"Thanks, man. I'll keep you posted on what Jaedon turns up." They talked a few minutes more. Then Omar drove home and called Jaedon.

Monday morning, he was seated in Jaedon's office, listening to Alonzo.

"This photo was last week, a day before Roland's arrest. You can see him handing her an envelope."

And two days after that story ran, Omar thought grimly. Two days after he made the biggest mistake of his life. He handed the photo back. "Since she works for the Grays, Malcolm said he and his brother would handle her."

"If the police can get a confession out of her, it would be easier to nail Roland's butt to the wall," Jaedon said.

"Yeah, let's hope." That still didn't get him any closer to reconciling with Morgan, but he wasn't giving up.

Morgan stopped short at the large floral arrangement sitting in her office when she arrived on Monday. Her family was going overboard. Rounding the desk, she plucked the card off and read.

You are my heart.
Omar

Her eyes slid closed. Why was he doing this? She missed him, *missed* him. She reread the card. What was she going to do? Tucking the card into her jacket pocket, she moved the arrangement to the small conference table and sat in her chair. She had agreed to continue working for the company at least until the end of the year, and she was on solid ground with her new job. Her commission from Omar's contract gave her a window of comfort.

By late morning, she had made a dent in the paperwork that had piled up while she was gone. Her head came up when a knock sounded. She smiled. "Hey, guys. Are you supposed to be the welcome back committee?" Her smile faded. "What is it?" She studied her brothers' grim expressions. Malcolm closed the door, and then he and Brandon took the chairs across from her desk.

"Is something wrong with Dad...or Mom?" Morgan came to her feet.

"They're fine," Brandon said. "Sit down, sis."

She gave a relieved sigh and slowly lowered herself back down.

"We know who leaked that story about Omar's contract," Malcolm said. "He came to see me last night and showed me a photo." He handed her his phone.

Frowning, she took the phone. She brought her hand to her mouth and stared in disbelief. "*Evelyn* and Roland? But how did she—" Morgan remembered the day she found Evelyn standing over her desk. "Oh, no. This is my fault."

Brandon shook his head. "This isn't your fault."

"It is. I left my notes on the desk."

"Every employee here signs a confidentiality statement when they're hired. She knew the rules. And she was paid twenty thousand dollars. That is a crime and we'll be pressing charges."

"What!" Morgan jumped from her chair.

Malcolm sighed. "You need to calm down, Morgan."

"And *you* need to pray I don't caress her face with my fist when I see her." She charged around the desk.

Malcolm hopped up, wrapped his arms around her and blocked the door.

"Get out of my way, Malcolm! And let me go!"

"No can do, sis. Dad called the police, and she's probably been taken in already."

She wrenched away from him and slammed her hand on the desk. Her chest heaved and her heart pounded in her chest. She wanted to strangle the woman. Bracing her hands on the desk, Morgan closed her eyes drew in several calming breaths. All this drama and for what? "Did she say why she did it?" When neither Brandon nor Malcolm answered, she opened her eyes and angled her head in their direction. The two brothers shared a look.

Finally Brandon answered. "She was angry because she had to be transferred to you and didn't like someone younger than her telling her what to do."

"She tried to wreck my life because I'm younger than her," she said, almost in disbelief.

"And Roland was trying to find a way to get back at you and Omar. Apparently he wasn't too thrilled by that set-down you gave him," Malcolm added.

"How do you know all this?"

"When we showed her that picture and told her she was looking at some jail time, she started singing like Jill Scott," Brandon offered. "My guess is that she's probably going to throw Roland under a bus and back it over him. Added to the other charges against him, he'll definitely be looking at some jail time."

"I hope so."

Brandon rose to his feet. "You going to be okay?"

Morgan nodded.

He placed a kiss on her forehead. "I'm going to check with Dad. I'll call you later."

"Okay."

When he left, Malcolm ran a comforting hand down her back. "Just so you'll know, Omar made sure the reporter will correct the story."

"How is he?"

"About as miserable as you," he said with a chuckle. "This is why I'm staying single." He shuddered.

She rolled her eyes. "Go home."

He laughed. "I'm just sayin'. Way less drama." He hugged her. "You coming on Sunday?"

"Have I ever missed a home game?" It would be the first preseason game.

"No, but you didn't have a vested interest in one of the players, either." He winked and exited.

Morgan leaned against her desk. She needed to make a decision about this relationship soon.

By the time Sunday rolled around, she was still confused about what to do. She loved Omar, but fear had a grip on her. If it didn't work out, she didn't think she would be able to take it. She didn't want to feel that kind of pain in her heart again.

Brandon and Justin were already in their seats when she arrived. She greeted them with hugs. "Where's Siobhan?"

Justin laughed. "She said she wasn't sitting out here in this heat."

"Yep, that's Vonnie," she said, joining in his laughter. The smile froze on her face when her gaze connected with Omar's out on the field.

"Hmm, looks like another Gray is about to take the plunge," Justin said.

Morgan's face heated. Thankfully, the game started. Omar was playing terribly. She groaned when he missed another easy pass. Near the end of the second quarter, she told Brandon and Justin she'd be back and made her way through the crowd of people headed to the concession stands.

Flashing her credentials to a security guard, she was able to gain access to the restricted area. She caught one of the Cobras staff members she knew before he entered the locker room. "Hi, Joey."

"Morgan," he said with a smile. "I haven't seen you in a while. I hear congratulations are in order."

"Thanks. Can you do me a favor?"

"Anything for you, beautiful."

She handed him a folded piece of paper. "Can you give this to Drummond?"

"I'll pass it along," he answered and pushed through the doors.

"Thanks." It was time to settle this, one way or another.

Chapter 20

"Hey, Drummond."

Omar turned toward the voice.

"Got a note for you."

"Thanks." Curious, he unfolded the paper.

I didn't work my butt off to get you a once-in-a-life-time contract for you to be playing like a kindergart-ner touching a football for the first time. Get your head in the game, Drummond. Meet me outside the locker room.

He chuckled. That was his Morgan. The vise around his heart loosened.

In the second half, Omar played like a man possessed and logged one hundred five yards and two touchdowns. Afterwards, he had postgame interviews at the podium. He answered question after question and was anxious to be done. He spotted Morgan standing in the back, promptly lost his train of thought and had to ask the reporter to repeat the question.

"There are rumors that you and your new agent have parted ways. Is that the truth?"

Holding Morgan's gaze, he said, "That's not the truth at all. I'm very happy with my agent and see no reason to change."

"There's been some speculation that there's a new lady in your life. Is there a reason you're keeping her a secret?"

"It's not a matter of keeping secrets. It's about keeping my personal life *personal*. Any other questions?" He paused for a few seconds then stood. *Finally!* It took another ten minutes before he found Morgan. "Hi." She wore a pair of shorts and a fitted tee that clung too enticingly to every curve. Dressed this way, she didn't look like an agent, but she did look like the woman he loved. And he did love her more than he ever thought possible.

"Hi."

"How are you?"

"Okay."

"Congratulations on signing Noah and Kent."

"Thanks."

They fell silent. "You'd probably sock me if I kissed you right now."

"You're probably right." A smile peeked out.

"Then you'd better start talking or I'll just deal with the consequences."

"I don't know where to start. I thought I could get over you, but it's not working."

"I'm glad because I'll never be over you. What can I do to make this work? I can't give you up. You own my heart, Morgan."

"How do I know this won't happen again? What's to say the next time you see something questionable, you won't believe me? I can't go through this again," Morgan whispered with tears in her eyes.

Omar's heart ached seeing the pain reflected in her eyes, and he shoved his hands in his pockets to keep from reaching for her. "Let me follow you home and we'll talk there. I want to hold you in my arms so bad it hurts."

"Okay."

"I'll be there as soon as I can, sweetheart." He watched until she disappeared into the thinning crowd.

An hour later, he was on her doorstep.

"Come on in." She had changed into another pair of shorts and a tank top and was barefoot.

Omar shut the door behind him and held out his arms. "I need to hold you, baby." She came to him and he enfolded her in his embrace. He swept her into his arms, carried her to the living room and sat on the couch with her on his lap. Their eyes held, and he covered her mouth in a tender kiss. A rush of emotions washed over him—relief, joy, peace and most of all, love. Having her in his arms again was like a balm that soothed his heart. He couldn't stop touching or kissing her. It felt like months had passed since the last time they were together.

Morgan's hands were just as busy. She and Omar were a tangled mass of hands and lips tasting, exploring and feeling.

"It's so good to hold you again," he murmured.

"I missed you holding me."

At length they came up for air, but he kept her in his lap and rested his cheek against the top of her head.

"I'm sorry," she said sometime later.

He lifted his head. "About?"

"I left my notes on your contract on my desk."

"That didn't give her the right to do what she did. It's not your fault. This was all Roland's doing. From what Jaedon told me, Evelyn took a plea in exchange for her testimony. She may still have to do some time, but with all the other charges, Roland will be going away for a long time. He told me that he talked to you, too."

"I warned Roland what would happen if I saw one thing. He must have thought I was playing."

Omar chuckled. "That's my girl. Well, now he knows for sure."

"I don't want to talk about them anymore."

"Me, either." He would much rather have been making love to her, but tamped down on his desire because they needed this time just to be together.

Morgan stared up at him. "Can we make a pact to always ask questions before jumping to conclusions?"

"Absolutely." He sealed the deal with a kiss.

"What are you doing tomorrow since there's no practice?"

"I was thinking I could take you over to the restaurant to meet my parents. We'd have to go a little earlier, say five-thirty or six, so I can get home."

"That's fine. No late nights for you. I'll be making sure you're not breaking curfew. I'm glad the Cobras are one of the teams who don't hold camp in the middle of nowhere anymore." Since building a state-of-the-art facility three years ago, upper management felt the players still bonded during the fourteen-hour days.

"So am I."

"Speaking of curfew…"

"I have a little more time." He wanted to pack her up and take her to his house. But doing that would guarantee a sleepless night, so he contented himself with holding her. They would have plenty of time to play catch-up.

"I'm glad you agreed to come with me tonight," Omar said Monday evening.

"Please. I wasn't missing out on a chance to taste this famed barbecue."

"Let me get my kiss now, because once we step out of the car, you'll have me on lockdown."

Morgan laughed and stroked a finger down his chest. "You act like you don't get kisses…and *more*."

He grasped her hand and brought it to his lips. "Mmm, the *more* might get you naked in the backseat of this truck right now."

The thought, as scandalous as it was, sent pinpoints of desire shooting through her. "We need to get out of this truck." She reached for the door handle.

"Yeah, yeah. And take your hand off that handle." He got out and came around to open her door.

She pulled him down for a slow, drugging kiss. "That ought to hold you for a while." She strutted off toward the entrance.

Omar groaned and caught up to her. "You little tease." He held the door open.

Morgan was enveloped in the warm, cozy atmosphere the moment she crossed the threshold. The people who worked there seemed to be enjoying themselves as much as the patrons. An older woman conversing with some diners turned their way, and her face lit up. She hurried over and smothered Omar in a big hug.

"Hi, baby. I'm so glad to see you."

Omar chuckled. "You saw me less than two weeks ago, Mom." To Morgan he said, "Morgan, this is my mother, Miriam Drummond. Mom, Morgan Gray."

"It's a pleasure to meet you, Mrs. Drummond."

"I'm so pleased to finally meet you, Morgan. Welcome to Miriam's Place. Let's get you two seated." She hooked her arm in Morgan's and led her away.

Morgan glanced over her shoulder at Omar, who shrugged. Mrs. Drummond reclaimed her attention.

"I can't believe it has taken Omar this long to bring you to meet us."

"Um…well, we haven't—"

She gave a short bark of laughter. "My dear, I know young love when I see it." She gestured to a booth. "I'll be right back."

When Omar joined her, she asked, "What did you tell your mother about us?"

"I didn't get a chance to tell her anything. She figured it out."

Before she could reply, Mrs. Drummond approached with an older gentleman who resembled Omar and his brother. "Is that your father?" The man stood over six feet and had the same deep bronze coloring. He had a few lines bracketing his face and some added girth around the waist but was still strikingly handsome.

"Hey, Dad."

"Bobby, this is Morgan Gray," his mother gushed before Omar could make the introduction.

Morgan stifled a laugh at the expression on Omar's face.

"Nice to meet you, Morgan."

"It's nice to meet you, too, Mr. Drummond."

"I've never met a lady sports agent."

She didn't know how to respond to this man staring at her in awe.

"Dad, Mom, can we get a couple of menus? Morgan and I don't have a lot of time."

"Oh, yes, yes. Sorry. I need to get back to the kitchen," his father mumbled.

"I'll get those menus," his mother said.

Omar shook his head. "Sorry about that."

Morgan smiled. "My parents will probably be the same way, especially my mother. She wants to know when I'm going to invite you to our family dinner. With your hectic schedule, it probably won't happen until after the season ends. Or we can always do it on the bye week."

"Nope. Can't do it. I'm taking you up to the cabin."

"You don't hear me complaining." A woman came and handed them menus. It took Morgan only a minute to choose. "I'm ready." She ordered the ribs, macaroni and cheese and green beans, while he chose grilled salmon, a baked yam and steamed vegetables. Despite the crowd, it didn't take very long for their food to arrive. She said a quick blessing and dove in.

"What do you think?"

"These ribs are *so* good. You know how to cook these?"

He grinned. "I do indeed."

"In that case, I'll stay with you forever." A strange look crossed his face, and she realized what she'd said. "Aren't you going to eat?" She could feel him watching her but kept her eyes focused on her food.

His mother came back near the end of the meal. "How was everything, Morgan?"

"It was delicious."

"Glad to hear it. I have a special dessert prepared just for you."

"Oh, Mrs. Drummond, you didn't have to go through all that trouble."

"Believe me, it's no trouble at all," she said with a smile and sashayed off.

"Your mom is so sweet."

"She's the best."

Morgan glanced over her shoulder and saw his mother coming, holding one plate. "You're not eating dessert? I don't want to eat by myself."

"If you can't finish it, I'll help you."

"Promise?"

"Yes."

"Here you go, dear." Mrs. Drummond sat the plate down, smiled and strolled off.

Morgan went still, and her pulse skipped. In the center of the dessert plate sat a black velvet box. "Omar."

"Open it, baby."

She reached for the box with trembling hands and flipped the top up. She gasped softly. "It's beautiful." A lover of diamonds, she recognized the radiant-cut solitaire perfectly perched in the center, surrounded by two rows of round diamonds.

Omar came around and slid in next to her. "I love you, Morgan Gray. All that I am, all that I do and all that I have is wrapped up in you. Every place in my heart belongs to you. You are my everything, baby. Marry me."

The tears were flowing before he could finish the words. "Yes." He slid the ring on her finger and kissed her. A loud cheer went up. Morgan jumped and turned around. "Oh my God. My whole family is here." She buried her face in his chest.

"I figured we might as well turn this into a big old engagement party while we have the chance."

"I'm gonna kill Malcolm."

The rumble of his laughter vibrated against her cheek. "You said that the first day I came to your office."

Her head came up, and they smiled. They were bombarded with congratulations and hugs from both families, and she even had a chance to meet his brother, niece and nephew. Rashad didn't stay long because of the crowds, but it made her feel special that he'd come. "We can't stay here all night."

"I don't plan to. I'm taking you home, and then I'm going to make love to my future wife."

"I'll try not to keep you out too late. You owe me a rematch with 'Madden,' but I think I'll wait until we go to the cabin." She leaned over and whispered, "Because this time you're going to lose, and I plan to make you scream my name."

Without a word, Omar grabbed her by the hand, mumbled some hasty goodbyes and hustled her out to the truck.

He didn't say anything during the entire drive, but the tense grip he had on the steering wheel and his slightly labored breathing let her know he had a tight rein on his control and was about to snap. When they arrived at her house, he jumped out of the truck and nearly dragged her to the front door. Before she made it in the house good, his mouth came down on hers...*hard.* He kissed her greedily, his tongue thrusting deep. They never made it past the front door. Somehow, through her haze of desire, she heard the slide of his zipper and the tearing of a package.

He hiked up her dress and lifted her into his arms. Morgan wrapped her legs around him as he placed her against the door. His smoldering gaze locked on hers. Omar pushed her panties to the side and drove into her with one long stroke, burying himself to the hilt.

Morgan shuddered and closed her eyes. "I love you, Omar."

"I love you, Morgan. You are my heart."

Epilogue

Late March

"Relax, Omar. Everything is going to be just fine." Morgan chuckled as he ran around the center for the fiftieth time, checking and rechecking to ensure all was ready for the grand opening of the mental health center scheduled in a few minutes.

"I know, I know. What time is it?"

She shook her head and slid her arms around his neck. "It's three minutes past the last time you asked. Baby, it's all done. We're ready." She pressed a kiss to his lips.

Omar smiled. "Have I told you how much I love you?"

"You might have mentioned it a time or two, but I never tire of hearing it."

"Thank you for marrying me."

"It was the best decision I've ever made." They had gotten married last month right after football season ended and the Cobras had won the Super Bowl. "Although I'm still waiting on this fabulous honeymoon you promised me."

"And it will be. A seven-day Alaskan cruise, two weeks in Brazil and a week at our cabin sounds pretty fabulous to me."

"I can't wait. Who's up in 'Madden'?"

Omar made a show of thinking. "I don't remember."

"That's because I am," Morgan said with a laugh. She leaned up, intending to give him a quick kiss, but he cupped her face in his big hands and took over, sliding his tongue between her parted lips.

"Ahem."

They sprang apart.

Bryson stood behind them, smiling. "Can you two new-lyweds knock it off? You're making it hard on the rest of us single folks."

"Sorry," Morgan said. "Is it time?"

"Yep."

She smiled up at Omar and placed her hand in his. Together they went out front. After a few welcoming speeches, she handed him the large scissors to cut the ribbon that had been stretched across the door.

"I want us to do it together." He placed his hands over hers and counted to three, and they cut it in half.

Cheers went up, and people streamed in to get the first look at what was sure to become a beacon for veterans. Both their families had come to support them. She smiled and took pictures until her cheeks hurt. As the crowd died down, she spotted a family coming up the walk. She tapped Omar on the arm. "Look who's here."

His eyes misted as he and Rashad shared a rough hug.

"Thought I'd come out and see what you've got. No drugs, though," Rashad said.

"No drugs." Omar introduced Rashad to one of the psychologists, and the two went off to talk. Serena gave Morgan and Omar a strong hug. Then she and the kids followed Rashad.

"I can't believe he came. This is…"

"It's beautiful. I am so very proud of you, Omar Drum-mond." They stood arm in arm, and Morgan thought over everything that had happened since she'd said yes to rep-resenting him. She now had six clients and had quit her job. Roland was serving ten years for embezzlement. All of his assets had been sold and the proceeds used to repay Omar and the other two athletes he'd stolen from. Evelyn had gotten eighteen months. She glanced up at her husband. He would be starting his doctoral studies in the fall. Morgan never thought she could be this happy. Life was good. *Real* good.

* * * * *

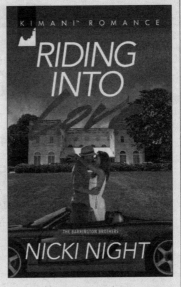

REQUEST YOUR FREE BOOKS!

2 FREE NOVELS
PLUS 2 *FREE GIFTS!*

KIMANI™
ROMANCE

Love's ultimate destination!

KROM15

Turn your love of reading into rewards you'll love with
Harlequin My Rewards